LASSOS and LACE

Books by Jody Hedlund

McQuaid Legacy: Healing Springs Ranch
Spurs and Sparks
Broncos and Ballads
Lassos and Lace
Horseshoes and Honeymoons

Noble Ranch
The Forever Cowboy
The Favored Cowboy

High Country Ranch
Waiting for the Rancher
Willing to Wed the Rancher
A Wife for the Rancher
Wrangling the Wandering Rancher
Wishing for the Rancher's Love

Colorado Cowgirls
Committing to the Cowgirl
Cherishing the Cowgirl
Convincing the Cowgirl
Captivated by the Cowgirl
Claiming the Cowgirl: A Novella

Colorado Cowboys
A Cowboy for Keeps
The Heart of a Cowboy

To Tame a Cowboy
Falling for the Cowgirl
The Last Chance Cowboy

A Shanahan Match
Calling on the Matchmaker
Saved by the Matchmaker
A Wager with the Matchmaker
Marrying the Matchmaker

Bride Ships: New Voyages
Finally His Bride
His Treasured Bride
His Perfect Bride
His Unforgettable Bride

Bride Ships Series
A Reluctant Bride
The Runaway Bride
A Bride of Convenience
Almost a Bride

Orphan Train Series
An Awakened Heart: A Novella
With You Always
Together Forever
Searching for You

Beacons of Hope Series
Out of the Storm: A Novella
Love Unexpected
Hearts Made Whole
Undaunted Hope
Forever Safe
Never Forget

Hearts of Faith Collection
The Preacher's Bride
The Doctor's Lady
Rebellious Heart

Michigan Brides Collection
Unending Devotion
A Noble Groom
Captured by Love

Historical
Luther and Katharina
Newton & Polly

Knights of Brethren Series
Enamored
Entwined
Ensnared
Enriched
Enflamed
Entrusted

Fairest Maidens Series
Beholden
Beguiled
Besotted

Lost Princesses Series
Always: Prequel Novella
Evermore
Foremost
Hereafter

Noble Knights Series
The Vow: Prequel Novella
An Uncertain Choice
A Daring Sacrifice
For Love & Honor
A Loyal Heart
A Worthy Rebel

Waters of Time Series
Come Back to Me
Never Leave Me
Stay With Me
Wait for Me

A HEALING SPRINGS RANCH NOVEL

LASSOS and LACE

JODY HEDLUND

NORTHERN LIGHTS PRESS

Lassos and Lace
Northern Lights Press
© 2026 by Jody Hedlund
Jody Hedlund Print Edition
ISBN 979-8-9998627-0-9

Jody Hedlund www.jodyhedlund.com

All rights reserved. No part of this book may be reproduced, stored in a retrieval system, or transmitted in any form, or by any means, electronic, mechanical, photocopying, recording or otherwise, without prior permission of the author.

This is a work of fiction. All characters are products of the author's imagination. Any resemblance to actual events or locales or persons, living or dead, is entirely coincidental.

Cover Design by RoseannaWhiteDesigns.com

1

"I'm running a fever of 102 degrees, Emberly." The voice on the other end of the phone was groggy.

"Of course you can't come in. I understand." Pacing her office, Emberly McQuaid tried to summon compassion for her employee, but all she felt was panic.

"I'm so sorry." Dwight's apology was drowned out by a fit of hacking that sounded like a barking dog.

Emberly halted at the window overlooking the front of the Healing Springs lodge. A light snow was lazily falling at midday, adding to the several inches that remained from last week. In the high country of Colorado, they always had plenty of snow, but a fresh dusting would make everything especially pretty for their incoming important international guests.

She pinched the bridge of her nose, closed her eyes against the wintry landscape, and drew in a breath.

Dwight was her best ranch ambassador, the most

polished, the most experienced, and the most knowledgeable. He was also mature, cultured, and professional—all the things that were important for being the private concierge for Mr. Milton, the president of Europe's largest and wealthiest bank, KWB—Karltenberg World Bank.

What would she do without Dwight?

Emberly opened her eyes to her reflection staring back from the window. Her long red hair was pulled into an elegant chignon, her slender face was taut, and her brown eyes were wide with desperation. "You need to take care of yourself, Dwight. That's what matters."

She meant it. She wanted Dwight to feel better. He was a good employee, and it wasn't his fault that he'd come down with the flu on the day the bank president and other executives of KWB Group were arriving.

"Maybe I'll be better by tomorrow." Dwight sniffled, then sneezed so loudly that Emberly held the phone away from her ear.

"I hope for your sake you do feel better tomorrow." She mentally tallied the list of available employees who could fill in for Dwight. She had a crew of twelve ambassadors. Half were already assigned to other important guests. The remainder were paired up with two—and in some cases, three—of the KWB Group's board members.

The truth was, she had no one to spare for Mr.

Milton—especially not anyone as qualified as Dwight.

"I'm sure with some rest and plenty of Nyquil," Dwight said through more sniffling, "I'll be back to myself in no time."

"I'll have Chef Vivalda send over his chicken noodle soup for you."

"Thank you." Dwight's voice held a note of weariness.

Had she been working him too hard? How long had it been since any of her ambassadors had taken a day off? Now that January was halfway done, had it been three weeks? Maybe four?

She held back a sigh of frustration aimed at herself. "You need the break, Dwight."

"But I know how important this event is to the ranch—"

"People are always the priority." The words fell out effortlessly—words drilled into her by her dad. His philosophy was that people were more important than programs, and that included employees as well as guests. Of course she felt the same way. But with the KWB Group visiting them for the first time, this was an opportunity to finally promote Healing Springs Ranch on a worldwide level. Even if Karltenberg was only a small country in Europe, it was still one of the wealthiest and home to the world-famous bank, and the recognition would make their ranch a renowned destination.

Already, it was one of the most luxurious vacation spots in the United States, attracting celebrities and the wealthiest Americans. The ranch had reservations booked at least a year in advance for every available room, cabin, and house.

But with an international stamp of approval, they would gain more attention and popularity. In doing so, they could finish earning the multimillions needed to purchase an adjacent area of land in the foothills, which had recently gone on the market. Both her dad and her oldest brother Tyler already had plans for that land, and they were excited about the new possibilities.

Emberly couldn't let them down. KWB Group's experience had to be excellent in every way, and she'd been planning each detail over the past few weeks to make sure their stay was perfection. That included making sure the ambassadors were assigned to the right people.

"Maybe you can pair Mr. Milton with a group of his friends?" Dwight's suggestion ended with another spurt of coughing.

She managed to say goodbye to him while at the same time texting a request to Chef Vivalda for the soup. Then she tossed her phone onto her desk, dropped into her chair, and surveyed the spreadsheets she'd printed.

Was there another group the president of the bank could join?

She read through the lists, then shook her head. From

all she'd learned about Mr. Milton and the discussions she'd had with Tyler and other staff, the middle-aged man was high maintenance and needed a one-on-one ambassador at his disposal.

After all, the ranch was known for its luxury concierge service to every family or couple who visited. The ambassadors contacted the guests three weeks before their visit to discuss and plan their desired itinerary. The ambassador reached out again a week before the arrival to touch base and make any updates. Then once the guests arrived, the ambassador made sure the visit went smoothly.

Not only did the ambassadors provide warm hospitality, but they also helped guests get the most out of their visits, scheduling activities from among the eighteen offered in the winter and the twenty-five available the rest of the year.

Yes, Mr. Milton needed his own personal ambassador, and if Dwight couldn't do it, she had only one other option left. She would have to take on the duties herself. She'd worked as an ambassador for a few years, and she knew the duties of an ambassador better than anyone else.

At twenty-five years of age, she might not be as experienced, knowledgeable, or cultured as Dwight, but she always acted professionally with guests and could pull strings to allow Mr. Milton to do anything he wanted.

In addition, she could speak several languages. She

might have failed out of college, but at least languages came easily to her, and she knew enough German to be able to converse with Mr. Milton in his native tongue.

Taking on the ambassador role for the week would mean delegating many of her responsibilities as event manager to her assistant. But Karen would do just fine. She had been doing the job long before Emberly had taken over, and knew every vendor, every supplier, every staff member, and every aspect of the ranch. She managed well, kept events flowing smoothly, and always took care of the logistics.

In fact, Dad had offered the event manager position to Karen first. But the single mom with two teenagers had turned down the promotion because she didn't want it taking away from her time with her sons.

Emberly felt like she was constantly having to prove she was capable of the job, that she hadn't just gotten it by default or because of her family. She'd done her best to create memorable and elegant events for each client, carefully lining up only the very best decorators, entertainers, activities, and transportation. She'd learned to make each event perfect, including seating arrangements, schedules, and even menus. She'd also shown herself to be financially savvy, keeping within budgets but still providing the best of everything.

Even with all her efforts, she knew staff still gossiped about her.

Expelling a long sigh, Emberly stood and smoothed a hand down her navy suit coat and matching pencil skirt. She'd taken extra care with her appearance today, even wearing heels, wanting to appear as qualified as possible when she met the KWB Group. But now, if she took on the role of ambassador, she would need to change into something more casual.

The walkie-talkie app on Emberly's phone dinged with an incoming announcement. "The KWB Group is arriving."

She glanced out the lodge window to see several BMW SUVs slowly making their way up the winding drive toward the lodge.

The group was early.

She wouldn't have time to run back to her cottage and change. Maybe that was for the best since she needed to make a good first impression on Mr. Milton. If he knew she was the event manager and that she was taking on his ambassador role personally, hopefully that would make him feel more special.

She freshened her makeup, made sure every hair was in place, rolled the lint off her suit, then lightly spritzed on more perfume. On her way out of her office, she stopped to talk to Karen about filling in for Dwight. Karen agreed that doing so was the right decision and assured Emberly she would take care of everything else for the week.

As the BMWs came to a halt in front of the lodge, Emberly waited with the ambassadors just inside the doors to welcome the group, her spreadsheets in hand.

The lobby was quiet, since most of the other guests were either still doing a morning activity or eating lunch. A large fire in the massive fireplace on the opposite wall crackled in the silence. Surrounded by stone from floor to vaulted ceiling, the fireplace with its long mantel was central to the lobby. Cozy leather chairs and couches were positioned beside side tables with log pedestals and glass tops. A chandelier made of antlers hung low and provided a warm and welcoming glow.

A guest services counter lined the opposite wall, with the managerial offices located on the rest of the first floor through the door behind the counter. The back wall of the lobby contained sliding glass doors and a patio that overlooked the lodge waterfall and Badger River. Eight suites filled the second floor of the lodge, and four more spacious suites took up the third floor. The Cliffside Dining Room was on the fourth floor, along with a wide balcony that allowed for a magnificent view of the waterfall from above.

The lodge, like everything else on the luxury ranch, had been built to wow the guests. Now, as Emberly watched the front door of the first BMW open, she could only pray that these guests truly would be wowed by the ranch.

A protection agent stepped out, surveyed the lodge and the road, then opened the back door of the BMW. A middle-aged man in a dark suit covered by a long wool coat slid out. He had a beard with threads of silver starting to show. His medium-brown hair had hints of silver too and was styled immaculately.

This had to be Mr. Milton, riding separately from those exiting the other BMWs. He didn't look like the picture she'd seen online. But sometimes such pictures were older and blurry and didn't do the real person justice.

She drew her suit coat around her more securely and then stepped forward so that the double glass doors opened. She exited onto the stone walkway that had just been shoveled and salted to keep it from being slippery for their guests.

Her heels clicked a staccato as she made her way toward Mr. Milton.

He was surveying the area too, just like his protection agent.

She hoped he liked what he saw so far. The rugged foothills covered in thick pine stood as a backdrop, as did the granite snow-covered peaks beyond. The lodge itself was surrounded by spruce and fir trees laden with snow. The other dwellings were tucked away, giving each home and cabin the feeling of privacy. The main barn and corral were the most visible buildings on the property, set in a cleared area. Like the rest of the structures, they were constructed of logs, giving them a rustic, natural aura.

"Welcome to Healing Springs Ranch, Mr. Milton." She halted as she reached the front BMW and held out her hand to the distinguished gentleman.

Mr. Milton took a rapid step back. "Pardon. I am Braun."

"Brown?"

"Yes. Braun." Speaking with a heavy German accent, the middle-aged man peered into the car. "I am the personal assistant of the . . . ah, what shall we say . . . ?"

"The CEO of KWB Group." Another man in a tailored blue suit began to climb out of the BMW. He was decidedly younger, with fair hair and no hint of gray, and wore Aviator sunglasses that hid his eyes but not his handsomeness—pronounced cheekbones, slender nose, his narrow chin and chiseled jaw covered with a neatly trimmed beard.

As the man straightened, he appeared to be over six feet, neither too tall nor too short. He wasn't bulky and brawny like her brothers, but he had a muscular build and clearly worked out regularly.

His air of confidence and authority belonged to a man with experience. If she had to pin an age on him, she'd guess he was in his thirties.

"Welcome to Healing Springs Ranch." She held out her hand to the man. "Mr. . . . ?"

Braun frowned and attempted to step in her way. "Nein, nein—"

The younger man dodged Braun and grasped Emberly's hand. "Max Berg. Call me Max." He offered her a broad smile that not only revealed perfect teeth but turned him from average handsome to heart-stopping.

She was glad she was able to stay composed. All those years of teasing from her four brothers had taught her how to hide her reactions, and she gave him nothing but a polite smile. She'd never made a habit of ogling guests, not even the stars who came. "Pleased to meet you, Max. I'm Emberly McQuaid, the event manager here at Healing Springs."

His grip was firm but didn't linger. Judging by the absence of a wedding band on his ring finger, he was single. As he released her hand, his gaze swept over her, stalling at her red hair and lingering over her face with a hint of surprise in his eyes, as if he hadn't expected someone like her to greet him.

"You can call me Emberly." She'd inherited the same beauty that had helped Mom win Miss Colorado many years ago—an elegant face with high cheeks, wide eyes, long lashes, and full lips, along with a body that could win the swimsuit portion of the competition.

Emberly had grown proficient at ignoring unwanted attention. She was even used to putting men in their place when necessary, and she wouldn't hesitate to do the same for this man if she needed to, no matter how important he might be.

As though realizing he was staring, he peered at the distant ski slopes on the outskirts of the tourist town of Healing Springs, named after the ranch, then shifted to take in the mountain range on the opposite side of Park County. Low winter clouds hung over them, hiding the peaks but creating an incredible scene with the wide valley spreading out and covered in snow. Light snowflakes drifted onto his head and shoulders.

"We weren't expecting the CEO of KWB Group," she said with a glance inside the car, half expecting Mr. Milton to slide out next. "But we're glad you're here."

She didn't know where she would put Max, since every room, cabin, and house was full. But she'd find someplace. She had to. And what about an ambassador for him? Would he need his own, or would she be able to place him with another group?

Her attention shifted to the other men exiting the vehicles, all of them looking the part of distinguished gentlemen in their suits. She couldn't put a cot in any of their rooms. It simply wouldn't do for this group.

She could feel Max taking her in again, so she offered a polite smile. "We'll make sure your time here is memorable."

"Good. Then I am glad I came." His sunglasses shielded his eyes, but there was no hiding his interest and the double meaning to his comment.

She searched the faces of the other guests, hoping to find Mr. Milton among them, but as far as she could tell, he wasn't there. "When should we expect Mr. Milton to arrive?"

"He is not coming."

"But isn't he in charge?"

"His wife took ill, and he asked me to come in his stead."

"I see." That would make the logistics easier. She could place Max in Mr. Milton's cabin and perhaps even shuffle the ambassadors around so that she wouldn't need to step into the role after all.

The ambassadors had followed Emberly and were milling around the other guests. One of them motioned at her.

"If you'll excuse me a moment," she said to Max.

For a few minutes, Emberly mingled among the others, answered questions, and made sure each of the staff was paired with the right guests. All the while, she scrambled to figure out which of the ambassadors to assign to Max. Perhaps she would need to ask him his preference.

Braun had been helping the protection agent unload the luggage from the back of Max's BMW. As the last suitcase was unloaded, Emberly started back toward Max.

Braun stepped up to Max's side and handed him a

briefcase. "Your Highness." Braun spoke in German.

Even so, the words were clear enough to Emberly. Was Max royalty?

"Just Max." Max frowned at his assistant and spoke in whispered German that she could barely hear. "Remember, this week I shall remain incognito to keep the paparazzi away."

She spun around and pretended to be busy with her clipboard and the spreadsheets she'd brought with her. Who exactly was this man?

Her mind spun as she worked to remember all the information she'd collected about the KWB Group, especially the CEO. Unfortunately, she couldn't remember much about the executive of the company because she'd focused most of her preparation on the president.

What she did know was that Karltenberg had a royal family who had been instrumental in starting the bank long ago, and they were still involved in its operations. She'd read a little about them as she'd familiarized herself with the country.

"I believe we are ready for our accommodations." Max spoke again, this time in English.

As she turned to face him, she forced herself to erase any and all signs of surprise and instead plastered on her most professional expression. "Of course."

He swiped off his sunglasses, revealing eyes that were

a silvery green like the sage that grew in the grasslands. "I hope that everything is in order."

Should she admit she could speak German and had heard the slip-up?

If she did so, would he leave because he was afraid she would call the paparazzi and alert them to his presence on the ranch? Even if she reassured him that she would keep his secret, he might make other arrangements, maybe even take the whole KWB board with him.

No, she had to act as though she didn't know about his royalty. There would be nothing wrong with that, especially because that's what he wanted.

She nodded at him. "Everything is in perfect order."

2

This remote place was just what he needed.

Max unbuttoned his suit coat, shrugged out of it, and tossed it over the back of one of the chairs in the cabin's cozy sitting room. He moved in front of the wood-burning fireplace that welcomed him with its warmth, and he held out his hands toward it while taking in the home that was to be his getaway for the next week.

Already, he could feel the stress of his life falling off his shoulders, like a knight shedding heavy armor. He was away from the battles with his father and mother and parliament. Maybe here he could finally think about what he ought to do with the looming deadline of his thirty-fifth birthday in just two months and especially the ultimatum to get married by that thirty-fifth birthday or abdicate his right as firstborn to become the next ruler of Karltenberg.

"The bedroom is rather small," Braun called in

German from the loft above the sitting room.

Winzig, who was tromping up the stairs with Max's luggage, halted.

Max waved a hand at his protection agent, who also served as his driver. "It will be fine for one week."

The lovely young woman who was overseeing their group stood near the door, having followed them to the cabin. "I do hope you're finding the cabin satisfactory." Without a coat and boots, she didn't seem to be in the least affected by the cold and snow, not even in her heels, which she'd worn as she'd led them down a secluded pathway away from the lodge to the cabin.

Braun responded before Max could. "We would like to move to one of the houses we passed. A cabin simply will not do. Especially one named Antelope."

The woman shifted the clipboard in her hand. "I'm sorry, but the houses are already booked for the week." She didn't sound too terribly sorry. Surely her lack of groveling was a good sign—a sign that she didn't know his identity.

It wasn't as if he was as recognizable as Prince Harry and Prince William. Not at all. Especially in a remote part of the United States like Colorado. But Max had gained press attention after he'd called off his engagement to the duchess, and ever since then, paparazzi had been hounding him. So far, however, no one seemed to realize that he was Prince Nikolaus Constantin Maximillian of the House of Karltenberg.

During all the correspondence with the board members of the KWB Group over the past week, he'd emphasized his desire for privacy and that they should only refer to him as Max and abstain from using his royal title. The gentlemen did most of the time anyway, so it wouldn't be too much of a switch for them. As long as Braun didn't make any more blunders, especially while speaking English, his identity would hopefully remain hidden.

"This is our best cabin and has two rooms," the woman was saying. "The loft has the canopy king bed, and the room on the first floor, behind the kitchenette, has a bunk bed. It has a cedar sauna as well as a hot tub. The porch is heated and provides some of the best views of the wilderness, and is just feet from the river."

Braun's brow furrowed. "It is not sufficient."

If Braun continued to ask for more, the woman would begin to suspect something was different about Max. Either that or consider him a spoiled elitist, which he didn't want to be true, even if it was at times.

Max leveled a stern look at his assistant. The cabin wasn't as glamorous or luxurious or big as he was accustomed to, but it was nice enough.

"We shall stay." He spoke first to Braun, then nodded at the woman. What had she said her name was? Kimberly? "Thank you, Kimberly."

"Emberly."

"Pardon me. Emberly." That was an odd name. "We are grateful for the accommodations." Especially because all the other men were staying in suites in the lodge with less privacy.

"You're welcome." She didn't move to leave. "If you have any needs during the week, you may contact me directly. I'll be your personal concierge, also known as an ambassador here at the ranch."

"There is no need for your service, especially since you have proven useless." Braun was starting down the stairs now that Winzig was up in the loft. "I am Max's personal assistant, and that is all he requires."

"No worries." Emberly lifted her chin at Braun. "You can continue to do all the complaining and pampering for Max, since that seems to be your arrangement . . . but my duties go well beyond that."

Braun halted midstride, his mouth open but not moving.

Max stopped rubbing his hands together in front of the fire and spun to face Emberly.

The woman crossed her arms and shifted to pin her gaze on him.

As with the introduction to her in front of the lodge, he was struck by her loveliness. Her hair was a vibrant red and styled in a fashionable knot. Her features contained a classic, timeless beauty. And her body was sculpture perfect, as if formed by a master artist.

She held herself with poise but also determination and didn't seem to be intimidated by the situation. She was likely accustomed to handling a wealthy clientele, since the ranch was designed to cater to the rich and famous.

"My duties," she continued politely but firmly, "include scheduling activities, planning outings, and ensuring that your stay here at the ranch is an unforgettable experience."

"That sounds grand." Max answered before Braun, wanting to prove that he wasn't as weak and helpless as this woman thought. "I am looking forward to a *private* week here."

Emberly nodded at his emphasis on the word *private*.

"*Very* private." Max lowered himself onto the nearest couch, which was filled with pillows bearing distinct patterns—one with diamonds and arrowheads, another with a barbed-wire pattern, and one with the skull of a steer. Apparently, the decorations were intended to provide a Western American feeling.

"I'll do my best to keep everything as private as possible." Emberly studied him. Was she attempting to discover what was motivating his need for privacy?

"Thank you. That is very accommodating of you."

"Since I was expecting Mr. Milton, I have an itinerary tailored to his interests. Sometime soon, after you have the chance to settle in, I'll sit down with you and you can share your interests, and I'll make up a new schedule of activities for you—one that ensures your privacy."

"Perhaps." He had briefly looked at the ranch's website and noticed the variety of activities offered—trail rides, ice fishing, snowmobiling, snowshoeing, cross-country skiing, ice skating, range shooting, and more.

However, he had more than enough work to keep him busy all week—especially the new high-profile client portfolios he needed to assess. He also had investment data to analyze, the plans for a Tokyo bank to scrutinize, and the growth advice of several senior advisers to examine.

The demands of his position were never-ending. Being CEO kept him busy day and night. And he hadn't planned on doing anything but working when he wasn't in meetings.

"Why not do something today?" Braun's eyes held his. Braun had just been telling him, as they'd pulled in through the main gate, that he should try to enjoy the time at the ranch and not work the whole time. "The first board meeting isn't until tomorrow morning."

Max glanced at his watch.

"You know you have the time." Braun started back down the steps again. "Besides, doing a few ranch activities will be good for you. You never make time for relaxation anymore."

Maybe he should take the time to enjoy the ranch just

a little, especially if it would ease the stress. A couple of activities wouldn't interfere too immensely with all he had to get done.

"Very well." He beckoned Emberly toward the plush armchair positioned beside the sofa. "Please sit. We shall arrange the activities now."

She took a look at her phone. Was she also taking note of the time? Or her schedule?

He had assumed she was available, but maybe he should have asked first. "Or we can wait—"

"No." She was already typing on her phone. "If you'll give me one moment to respond to messages from my staff, then we can proceed with the planning."

"Of course."

She cast a brief look his way. "Excuse me." Then she pushed open the door and stepped out onto the covered front porch of the cabin before closing the door behind her.

As soon as she disappeared from sight, Braun started tsking. "That woman is not respectful enough." He lapsed into German. "If only she knew who you are."

"This is how I want it, Braun." When most women discovered he was a prince, their whole demeanor changed with him, especially when they learned he was still single.

He could admit he had put off finding a wife when he was younger. First, he'd attended Cambridge, and his time there had been full of too many parties and too much reckless living. Once he had grown up a bit, he'd devoted himself to his career in finance and had gone to the University of Salzburg for his MBA.

After earning the degree, he'd immersed himself in the world of banking and investments. His primary focus had been expanding KWB to Asian and Middle Eastern countries. In the process, he'd multiplied the wealth of the bank exponentially, during which he'd become the youngest CEO the company had ever known.

By that time, the marriage deadline had already been looming. It wasn't a Karltenberg law that the heir apparent had to get married by thirty-five. But it was a tradition. If he couldn't find a wife by his upcoming birthday, then his father had asked him to step aside and allow his second-born brother to become the heir apparent. Parliament had been pushing Max to do so for the past year, primarily because Alex was already married and had three young sons. As a result, Alex would be able to carry on the lineage of the House of Karltenberg.

Alex wasn't as ambitious or outspoken and was a gentler soul with an artistic side. He was in charge of the Prince of Karltenberg Foundation, which helped maintain the family's castles, cultural assets, collections, and museums, and did a fine job of ensuring the future of the important historical and artistic artifacts that belonged to the royal family.

Alex had married when he was twenty-four, and now, at thirty-one, his oldest son was six years old, healthy, strong, and smart. Parliament liked Alex, liked his family, and liked the stability he brought to the royals—unlike Max, who, at thirty-four, was still unmarried, had no heirs, and had no prospects. Even his youngest brother Joseph, at twenty-eight, was engaged and planning a wedding to take place later in the year.

Over the past several years, Max had attempted to form serious relationships. Most recently, he'd tried for at least six months with Sarah, the Duchess of Bavaria. At twenty-three, she'd been a bit immature and hadn't liked him overly much but had stayed with him because she was enamored with the prospect of becoming queen.

His father and mother had been frustrated when he'd walked away from Sarah. While they understood he didn't want to enter a marriage that would make him unhappy, they were also upset that he wasn't doing more to make the relationship with Sarah work. They thought he should be focusing all of his attention on finding another woman who would make him happy, which was easier said than done.

Perhaps he had been rash to end his relationship with Sarah. Perhaps he should have considered marrying her regardless of his concerns. After all, he was far from perfect himself.

He understood his father's push. His father had just

turned sixty and wanted to appoint him prince regent and hand over the duties of ruling the country. His father would still remain head of state, but essentially, he wanted to retire from the many demanding responsibilities that came with being king.

However, he couldn't retire if he didn't know which son would take his place. Since Max was first in the line of succession, the choice was ultimately up to him. Whether he married or not, he could become the next king. Yet he also understood the dilemma and difficulties that would arise if he didn't marry and remained childless.

Max leaned his head back against the couch cushions. This was why he craved the solitude of this trip and why he'd agreed to come in place of Mr. Milton. He needed time to sort out all his options away from the constant pressure.

Suddenly feeling a swell of anxiety in his chest, he pushed to his feet. He'd been restless too oft of late, and he wanted to finally find peace and contentment. Yet even here in this rustic wilderness, peace and contentment seemed to be elusive, and the frustration inside was swirling faster.

He stalked across the room to the sliding glass door leading to the enclosed back porch. He opened it and stepped into a room that was filled with windows, allowing a panoramic view of the outdoors and the nearby river. A heater was blowing out warm air so that the room was pleasant. The furniture and decorations, like the rest of what he'd seen of the house, were also rustic-themed.

He stuffed his hands into his pockets and peered out at the river, which was frozen over on the edges but still held rushing water in the center. The snow on the pine trees made them bow low as if paying homage to the river. It was a spectacular vista, especially with the mountain peaks rising in the distance beyond the river.

What was wrong with him that he couldn't be happy here, even in this beautiful place?

"Max?" came a voice behind him.

He shifted to find that Emberly had joined him in the enclosed porch.

"Would you like to plan your schedule out here?" She started to close the door.

He actually didn't want to do any planning. He just needed to get out of the cabin and forget about the pressures for a short while. Maybe then he could settle his thoughts and plunge back into the mounds of work awaiting him. "Let us go for a hike."

She studied her clipboard and tapped a pencil against it. "I have a guide available tomorrow at one o'clock. I'll make sure you're the only one—"

"I should like to go now."

She shook her head. "The guide has already left with a group."

"You can be my guide."

"That's not one of my duties."

"I thought your duty was to ensure that my stay at the ranch is unforgettable?"

"Yes, but—"

"Then you shall take me on the hike yourself." He liked the idea the more he proposed it. "I did make it clear that I would like privacy, and having you guide me would be about as private as I could ask for."

Emberly lowered her clipboard and leveled a stern look at him. "Well, let me make something clear to you." Her voice had an almost sassy note to it that surprised him. When had staff talked to him in such a tone? He couldn't remember anyone, ever.

"My job is to arrange your activities," she continued, "not to do them with you." She cocked her head and braced one hand upon her hip as if daring him to defy her.

A strange thrill shot through him. Not only was this woman speaking freely with him, but she wasn't trying to impress him or defer to him or even show him courtesy. She was simply being herself.

He liked the interaction. In fact, he liked it a great deal. Perhaps this was what it was like to be an average person. Could he be that this week?

Yes. Having a week of being a regular man was just what he required. "What if I insist on having my personal concierge accompany me during my activities this week?"

"You can insist, but that doesn't change my duties."

"I shall pay you double your salary for the week."

"Absolutely not."

"Triple?"

"This isn't about the money."

"Four times the amount."

She released an exasperated sigh. "My father owns the ranch."

His thoughts came to an abrupt halt. That made sense. After all, she had introduced herself as a McQuaid. He didn't know much about the McQuaids except that the famous country music star, Brock McQuaid, called the ranch home. Not that Max was particularly fond of country music or a fan of Brock. However, Brock's engagement to supermodel Venus Vargas had recently been splashed across the front page of most major news outlets, and Max hadn't been able to avoid seeing the pictures of the happy couple.

Maybe Emberly was being truthful that she didn't need the money. The McQuaids likely were very wealthy. Even so, as a McQuaid, she probably knew the ranch better than almost anyone else and could do anything she wanted.

He couldn't hold back a smile. "The matter is settled."

She didn't smile back.

For a reason he couldn't decipher, he liked her attitude, liked her resistance. "That means you are the perfect one to accompany me this week. Since you have grown up on the ranch, who better than you to show me everything?"

"The trained guides are better."

"I disagree. Family is always more passionate and invested than a paid employee."

She narrowed her eyes upon him, but not before he saw that he'd hit on the truth. She needed this week with their group to go well. Even though she didn't necessarily want to act as his personal tour guide and accompany him to the various activities, she would do it for the ranch.

"I shall make the effort worth your while," he added. He wasn't sure why he was pushing her so hard when she clearly didn't want to do it. Perhaps because he was accustomed to getting his way. Perhaps because he appreciated a challenge and saw one in her. Perhaps because he already liked her for being so real.

She pressed her lips together.

The movement drew his attention there. She had a beautiful mouth with naturally full lips, the cupid's bow adding a pucker in the middle that looked like it would be delectable.

One of her brows quirked. "You're willing to strike a bargain?"

"Within reason."

"I'd love your group to spread the word about our ranch to your friends and colleagues."

"That will be no trouble."

"Fine. I'll go with you and be in charge of your activities."

His smile widened. "Then let us be on our way."

3

What had she gotten herself into?

Emberly's boots crunched along the pathway as she returned to Max's cabin. Through the snowy spruce branches, she spotted him already waiting outside, pushing back and forth in the log-framed porch swing, his laptop open in front of him.

She tugged at her beanie, pulling it so that it covered her ears. Then she zipped her black North Face parka higher.

Had she made a mistake in agreeing to this arrangement with Max? Essentially, she'd told him she would be exclusively available to accompany him wherever he wanted to go or assist him in whatever he wanted to do.

Did she want to be at his beck and call?

The good thing about it was that he had seemed reluctant to take time out of his work schedule to do activities. She'd seen men like him come to the ranch on business and then spend most of their time in a conference room. In reality, Max would probably do a couple of activities before getting busy with his work, and then her job entertaining him would be over.

He'd been right that she was proficient in all things having to do with the ranch. She knew this place better than most people, even her family. As the event manager, she had to stay on top of everything that went on. She not only hired and trained all the ambassadors and assigned them to incoming visitors but also arranged special events for businesses and oversaw reunions, weddings, celebrity stays, and more.

Even though she was a college dropout, she'd been trying to prove to her family that she could be successful without a degree. Here was her chance. All she had to do was play the role of tour guide to a prince for a week, and in exchange, he'd agreed to endorse the ranch on an international level. She hoped the KWB board members would also promote the ranch, but having a prince's words of praise would help even more.

Although Max had been ready to get out and explore and hike around the ranch right away, she'd told him she needed an hour to wrap up some miscellaneous details of her job. She'd popped into the office and told Karen about her arrangement with Max. Emberly hadn't mentioned Max was a prince, but she had indicated that the wealthy man had a great deal of influence, which would be a boost to the ranch.

After tidying up as many loose ends as she could, she'd gone to her cottage near the lodge to change into clothes more suitable for traipsing around.

Now, as she made her way toward Max, she tried to quell her irritation and talk herself into believing she would have fun showing him the ranch and helping him with various activities. How hard would it be to get him started on something and then to sit back and wait for him to finish? It would be like babysitting, except in this case, she would be taking care of a spoiled and rich grown man who needed a personal assistant to do anything of significance.

Her assessment was a tad harsh. From what she could tell so far, he was a decent man. She'd seen far worse—men who were rude and entitled and walked all over the ranch staff. At least Max had been respectful.

The snow had stopped, and only a light dusting covered the pathway. The trails that wound through the woods around the property would have more snow, but nothing that her sturdy hiking boots couldn't handle.

The question was, did Max have the right gear? Or was he expecting to hike around the ranch in his three-piece suit and expensive leather dress shoes?

Even if he wanted the privacy, she knew she needed to stay in places that were visible to other staff. It was the ranch's policy that employees, including ambassadors, avoid being alone with guests. Of course, there were times when that was impossible, but everyone was encouraged to stay professional and public.

As she stepped past the last of the spruce and started up the flagstone path to the cabin, Max slid her a quick glance as he typed on his laptop. "You look warmer than before."

"I am." A sweatshirt and leggings were her usual attire when she wasn't working, which wasn't often. But she had been making more time to see her dad after his fight against pancreatic cancer last summer. He'd been steadily gaining his strength back since he'd finished his last round of chemotherapy back in November.

Her dad had maintained good spirits and kept busy with low-level marketing for the ranch. But he still wasn't completely himself, and that was the hardest part—seeing his decline and not being able to do anything about it. All she really could do was cherish him and Mom better and not squander however many days together they were given.

Emberly paused at the cabin steps and took in Max wearing a different outfit—jeans, a sweater, a heavy parka similar to hers, and boots that would help his feet stay warm. So he did have the right clothing after all. No doubt his personal assistant did all Max's packing and made sure he had more than he needed for every possible occasion.

"Ready to see Healing Springs Ranch?" She forced cheer to her voice.

He paused in typing—probably responding to an email—and shifted to study her face with narrowed eyes.

Could he tell she wasn't thrilled with this new role he'd thrust her into?

Slowly, he closed his laptop and set it aside on the swing bench. Then he began to put on a pair of gloves. "I am extremely ready."

"Extremely?" She couldn't hold back a scoff. "You don't need to pretend to be exuberant with me."

"I am not pretending any more than you are. Who would not be *extremely* excited about seeing a real American ranch?"

"You. I doubt you get excited about much."

"I am enthusiastic about many things."

"Maybe enthusiastic about your work. But it's easy to see you don't take time for much pleasure."

"Then it's a good thing I have you to transform me, since you are so obviously eager about introducing me to your ranch."

Oh, he was good at sparring with words.

With a smug smile, he slid his sunglasses down from the top of his head, even though the cloud cover was still thick and gray. Did he hope to hide his true identity behind his sunglasses? It wouldn't work here. Wearing the glasses would have the opposite effect in drawing attention, especially when there wasn't even a hint of sunshine.

As Max loped down the stairs, she reached for his glasses, plucked them off, and then stuck them in one of the front pockets on his jacket.

His eyes widened, revealing the silvery green again, but this time they were filled with surprise, as if he hadn't expected her to be so bold.

She stuffed her hands into her coat pocket. "We're known for having celebrities who come here, so if you want to stay unnoticed, you'll need to try to blend in."

"Celebrities?" He arched a brow, his eyes suddenly sharp. "Is that what I am?"

Shoot. She wasn't supposed to know he was a prince. She couldn't forget that.

With a nonchalant shrug—or at least, she hoped it was nonchalant—she started back down the path. "I'm just saying that sunglasses are the surest way to make people *think* you're a celebrity, whether you're one or not. So to give you the private week you're hoping for, let's ditch them, okay?"

For a moment more, he was silent, then his footsteps thudded after her. "So, where are we going first?"

She paused at the end of the walkway and waited for him to reach her side. As soon as he did, with his protection agent a discreet distance away, she started forward again. "We'll hike around the ranch to an overlook. You'll get a good view of the land from there."

"Sounds perfect." He fell into step with her.

As they walked along the path, he surprised her by asking about Colorado's history as well as her family's history of the ranch. She'd thought he was being sarcastic when he'd mentioned being interested in the ranch, but his questions were genuine.

The truth was, she loved talking about her family's history, how her ancestors had originally come to the West in the 1860s to look for gold but had ended up ranching instead. Two of the original McQuaid brothers, Wyatt and Flynn, had built ranches on adjacent homesteads.

"Wyatt's firstborn son was Tyler McQuaid," she explained as she stepped up the rocky trail. "When he grew up, he married Flynn's daughter, Flora."

"He married a cousin?" Max didn't sound winded behind her, even though they'd reached a more strenuous portion with a steeper incline. "I did not realize Americans engaged in the practice of marrying cousins."

"We don't. But Flora wasn't really a McQuaid. Her mother, Linnea, was pregnant when her first husband died. During the long journey by covered wagon to the West, Linnea fell in love with Flynn and married him."

"And Flynn took care of her child?"

"Yes, Flynn never had any children of his own and adopted Flora, so she grew up a McQuaid. But technically, Tyler and Flora weren't related by blood."

"I see. So when the two married, they merged their ranches?"

"Merged and expanded." Emberly stepped carefully through the slushy snow to the next rock. "The ranch continued to grow over the years. Each new generation of McQuaids purchased more land in Park County, and now Tyler, my oldest brother, is hoping to do the same."

"Tyler?" Max was still right behind her, and every once in a while, she caught sight of his protection agent a dozen or so paces behind. "So your brother carries on the family name?"

"Every firstborn has been named Tyler Wyatt. But in order to make things less confusing, my dad goes by T.W., and Tyler's son—my eight-year-old nephew—goes by Wyatt."

"I understand the reasoning. Family names are important in my lineage as well."

She wanted to ask him about his name, but she also knew she could look it up online later and learn everything she needed. Besides, she didn't want him growing suspicious again.

She rounded a bend in the trail and climbed the last few steps to the top. As her feet reached the plateau and steady ground, she stopped and drew in a breath of the high-altitude air, which was crisp and cold and filled with the heavy scent of pine.

Max halted beside her and pulled in a breath too. He was obviously in good shape. And perhaps he was also used to the higher elevation, since from what she'd read, his country bordered the Alps.

He surveyed the ranch that spread out below them, snow-covered woodlands, open pastures dusted in white, and rugged ski slopes beyond.

"This reminds me of my home," he said quietly. "But more peaceful."

"It is peaceful." She'd always loved the view from this particular spot, since it gave such a sweeping scene of the ranch and the surrounding area. She'd hiked to the spot often while growing up. Whenever she'd come home during her two years at Colorado College in Colorado Springs, this was the place she'd been eager to visit first.

Max expelled a long breath. The stiffness in his shoulders seemed to ease just a little—a stiffness she hadn't noticed until now. His jaw was still rigid, his chin taut, his eyes narrowed with crow's feet at the outer corners. Even if he was spoiled, maybe he had more pressure on him than she understood.

His profile had a maturity and seriousness that made him look regal. Or maybe she only thought so because she knew he was royalty. Either way, with his blond hair, green eyes, and all-around perfect features, he was a good-looking man. It was hard not to acknowledge that fact.

And it was hard to believe that a man of his status and

handsomeness was unattached. Surely at the very least, he was engaged. She would have to research his love life later. But in the meantime, she was too curious to stay quiet. "It's a romantic spot."

Max slanted a sideways look at her.

"My dad proposed to my mom here."

He didn't respond.

"I told my ex-boyfriend that I wanted to get engaged here."

"Ex?"

She wasn't sure why she was telling Max such personal information—probably so that he'd share about himself in return. Regardless, she'd stepped over a professional line in divulging so much. But now that she'd started, she knew she had to give him a brief explanation. "Talking about engagement has that effect on some men."

"Sounds like a fine bloke." Max's voice turned sarcastic.

She'd dated Ryan for two years and thought they were moving in the direction of marriage. But when she'd brought it up, he'd claimed he wasn't ready. He'd also told her that her brothers were bullies, and he'd gotten tired of dealing with them.

"I apologize," Max said quickly. "I was out of line to speak that way."

She snorted softly. "It's all right. Ryan was a coward,

and I should have realized it sooner."

She could feel Max studying her, but she kept her gaze on the ranch.

"Was this a recent occurrence?" he asked, then shook his head. "No, I apologize again. 'Tis none of my business, and you may tell me so."

"No, I'm sorry for sharing so unprofessionally."

"You owe me no apology. I appreciate the sharing. And I am the one asking all the questions, am I not?"

"Would you like me to even things out and ask you a few questions in return?"

He paused, as though seriously considering the option.

"I'm teasing. I would never pressure you to share anything you don't want to."

"Thank you."

They both fell silent.

She could at least answer his last question about Ryan, couldn't she? "Last May."

Once again, she felt his gaze upon her.

"He broke up with me last May." She shifted to find Max's eyes filled with compassion. She faced him more directly, drawn to that compassion. "It was hard at the time." Especially because shortly after the breakup, Dad had been diagnosed with cancer.

Max didn't offer any platitudes, which she appreciated. Instead, he just held her gaze, the warmth there comforting her more than any words.

"It's been months, and I'm getting over him and moving on with my life."

"That is good."

Even though Ryan and his family lived in the area and owned one of the ski resorts, she rarely saw him anymore, only occasionally running into him when she was at a local event. Now, instead of feeling hurt whenever she was near him, she felt only anger that she'd wasted time being with him.

"I wish I could move on." Max's comment was quiet.

The comment sounded an awful lot like he'd just gone through a breakup too.

She wanted to ask him what he meant, but she'd just told him she wouldn't pressure him to talk about himself, and she wanted to prove she was right. "It takes time," she offered instead.

He sighed and stared ahead. "Time is one thing I do not have."

She sensed his turmoil just below the surface. Maybe that's why he worked himself so hard—so he could escape from a bad breakup. Or maybe there were other pressures as a prince that were difficult. What if being at the ranch could be a time of rejuvenation?

The name of the ranch originated from the tales of physical healing caused by the hot springs located here. But their philosophy was that healing could happen through self-care and relaxation as well as through the challenging activities they offered.

"A week here at the ranch could be just what you need to regain perspective."

"Perhaps." His voice turned wistful.

Something in his expression—the lostness—tugged at her. He had come to the ranch to work and oversee his company, but it was becoming clearer with every passing second that he could benefit from the healing the ranch provided.

To make that happen, she would have to stop feeling resentful about being his ambassador and instead put her heart into making the week meaningful.

Spending the time with him wouldn't be such a hardship, would it? So far, he'd been pleasant to talk to and had been kind and honorable. Even though he was privileged, he didn't seem like the type of man who would take advantage of her.

Yes, if he needed help, then what could go wrong by giving it to him?

4

No one here knew who he was. When was the last time he'd been able to go anywhere or do anything without being at the center of attention?

Max stepped up to the door of his cabin after the past several hours touring the ranch with Emberly then halted with one hand on the doorknob.

The freedom to be himself was incredible. Especially with Emberly.

The low light on the porch broke through the darkness of the evening and cast a glow over her where she stood at the bottom of the steps, bundled in her parka, her cheeks rosy, the tip of her nose a becoming pink, and her eyes bright.

"Dinner in Cliffside Dining Room at seven o'clock," she said again, taking a step back.

She'd been fantastic all afternoon, taking him around the ranch, giving him the history, showing him where all of the activities were located, hiking past the houses and cabins, visiting the barn and corral, introducing him to the horses, having coffee in the Brook Barn regardless of it being closed, showing him the waterfall from the balcony of the Cliffside Dining Room, even skirting past her family's home on the way back to his cabin.

He hadn't pressured her to take him inside, although he'd been tempted to ask her to introduce him to her family.

Emberly gave him a final nod. "I'll see you in the morning after your meetings."

In the morning? A strange disappointment wove through Max's chest. "You will not be at dinner?"

She'd started to turn but halted. "You're supposed to dine with the other members of your group tonight. We've prepared the banquet room for you. You'll have plenty of privacy, and I guarantee you'll enjoy the food and the view."

He didn't care about food or the view. He didn't care about dining with the other members, even though he had work to discuss. So what did he want? What was the disappointment about? Was it because he wasn't ready for his time with Emberly to come to an end?

During the time with her, he'd been able to push aside all the concerns of his life. Somehow, the stress had gradually fallen away. The worries about his future had faded in importance. Once he was alone again, all of that would come rushing back, even if he buried himself in work. And he didn't want it back. At least, not yet.

"I would prefer to have dinner in my cottage." Once he spoke, a plan began to take shape. "Is it possible to have the meal delivered here?"

"Of course. That's easy enough."

"Good. Please have four delivered. One for myself, Braun, Winzig, and you."

She opened her mouth to respond but then immediately closed it and frowned.

"Is that a problem? If so, I shall have Braun and Winzig go pick up the food."

She crossed her arms, still frowning. "The delivery isn't the problem, Max."

"Oh?"

"You can't assume I'm available to stay for dinner."

"Are you otherwise occupied?"

"No, but that's not the point."

"What is the point?"

"The point is that I'm not like Braun and Winzig. You can't dictate what I do. You need to ask me first."

"I see." She was right. He hadn't asked her and had instead simply expected her to do so, whether she wanted to or not. Maybe she was tired of him. Maybe she needed time to herself.

Had he always been so callous? He certainly had never considered Braun's or Winzig's needs. He had always presumed people would be willing to do whatever he suggested, mostly because no one had ever opposed him before.

"So you have no wish to dine with me tonight?" He didn't really have the time and should tell her not to worry about it, that he needed to work. But he also knew he could work later, after dinner. Even with jet lag, he could force himself to stay up and get through the most important issues.

She tilted her head and studied his face. "I'm not saying I'm opposed to having dinner with you." Her words were firm, but her eyes held a kindness that he liked. "What I am saying is that you need to ask. Nobody likes to be ordered."

Was he too accustomed to ordering people around? Yes, apparently he was. "I apologize. I would very much appreciate your company tonight over dinner, if you would be so gracious as to grant it to me."

She glanced down and seemed to be biting back a smile.

"Did I misspeak again?"

"No, you did beautifully." Her smile blossomed. It was the first she'd given him since their meeting earlier in the day. Her elegant features lit up, her eyes widened, and her teeth gleamed. The smile only highlighted how lovely she was, and it nearly took his breath away.

He dragged in a lungful of the cool evening air, not

sure why he was reacting so strongly to this woman's smile, except that a part of him already knew that her smiles were rare, and he'd been the one to put it on her face. If he'd done it once, could he do it again?

Without giving him the chance to try—and likely make a fool of himself in the process—she turned and began to walk away. "I'll be back for dinner."

For a moment, he could only watch her, but then he found his voice. "I would like you to stay."

She didn't break her stride.

He'd done it again. Ordered her, or at least assumed she'd harken to his wishes. He mentally slapped himself, then rushed to correct his mistake. "Would you please come inside and perhaps join me for a drink until dinner arrives?"

She stopped and tossed him a sassy look. "That's better, Max. You're a quick learner."

He couldn't keep from smiling. "Thank you."

"But no, I can't stay."

His delight fell away immediately, along with his smile. "Whyever not?"

She gave him a last look before continuing on her way. "I'll be back in an hour."

He wanted to say more, to ask her where she was going, what she was doing, who she was seeing. But the questions would be totally irrational and entirely out of line in this situation. Maybe even in all situations.

With a sigh, he watched her until she disappeared, then he entered the cabin and left the door open for Winzig, who had been waiting in the shadows of the porch.

At the table in the kitchenette, Braun had his monocular loupe in one eye and his stamp collection book spread out in front of him.

"Good evening, Your Highness," Braun stated in German as he hovered above one of the stamps. "Would you like to wear the red tie or blue to dinner?"

"Neither, since I am not going." Max shrugged out of his coat.

Braun immediately straightened in his chair, the single magnifier still in his eye socket. "You must. It's on the schedule."

"I have decided to dine in the cabin this evening." Max tossed off his gloves as Winzig entered and closed the door.

Braun pushed back from the table, stood, and crossed toward Max, his face creasing with worry, even with the loupe in his eye. "Are you unwell, Your Highness?"

"I am completely fine."

"I do not understand."

Max bent to unlace his boots. He didn't quite understand himself either. The bank was his life. He ate, slept, and lived for the bank and always had, but more so over recent months. When he wasn't at his desk at the main branch in Vollenstadt, he was traveling to the ancillary banks in other cities and countries, meeting with investors and other executives.

Even on the long flight over from Europe, he'd worked most of the way and slept only a little. After they'd landed in Denver, he'd spent the ride into the mountains on one conference call after another.

He honestly hadn't planned on spending the entire afternoon touring the ranch. He'd expected to be gone an hour so that he'd have time to work until dinner. But once he'd started hiking with Emberly, he'd stopped paying attention to his watch. He also hadn't cared that his phone had been vibrating in his pocket, accumulating messages to respond to in addition to everything else he needed to do.

He'd been too distracted by her and by the beauty of the land to let himself worry about anything.

Then she'd made a comment about being at the ranch that had struck a chord deep inside: *A week here at the ranch could be just what you need to regain perspective.*

What if she were right? What if he'd been using his work to escape from the increasing pressure of what to do about his future? What if he simply needed to be here at the ranch to rest and relax? Would it help him gain the perspective he needed for the monumental decision on whether to marry Sarah or abdicate the throne to Alex?

Braun stopped in front of Max and examined him

through his single magnifying lens, as if that could somehow unravel the confusion.

Max kicked off his boot. "I would like to enjoy an evening off, Braun."

"I am not opposed to it, Your Highness. I have repeatedly encouraged you not to work so hard. But . . ."

"But what?" Max slipped the other boot off and straightened.

Braun finally plucked the loupe from his eye. "But nothing, Your Highness. I am glad you intend to rest this evening."

"Thank you, Braun." Max started toward the stairway that led to the loft. "I should like to freshen up and change my garments before dinner arrives."

Braun, in the process of hanging up Max's coat, froze.

"What shall I wear?" Max asked. "Do I have anything else casual but nice?"

Braun didn't respond.

"I like this sweater. Perhaps one similar."

"'Tis the girl." Braun's voice rang out with conviction.

Max waved a hand, brushing aside Braun's comment. "She is good company. That is all." That *was* really all. He did not have time to become distracted by a pretty American woman on this trip. Not when his life was a speeding train that was hurtling toward his next birthday faster than the Eurostar.

"You like her," Braun said even louder.

"I barely know her." That wasn't true. After spending the afternoon with her, he had learned a great deal about her as a person. She came from a solid family who cared about each other. She was very good at her job and took her work at the ranch seriously. She was excellent with the employees and kind to the other guests they'd come across. She was knowledgeable and interesting to talk to.

Most importantly, she treated him like a regular bloke. Even just a few minutes ago, she hadn't hesitated to confront him about being demanding with her. Would she be so open and honest if she knew he was a prince?

He sighed. He probably ought to tell her. But what would that accomplish? She would start treating him differently, and he didn't want that. After getting a taste of what it was like to be normal, he didn't want things to change. For at least this week, he could enjoy being like everyone else, couldn't he?

It certainly wouldn't harm her to go on believing he was simply a rich man from a rich European family. After all, they would part ways when the week was over. He would return home. And they would never see each other again.

"Is she coming back for dinner?" Braun asked in a too-knowing way.

"She is." Max finished ascending the stairs to the loft. The sleeping quarters were more spacious than he'd expected, even with the king bed, which was made of the same pine logs as the other furniture. Two wide leather chairs took up one corner with side tables beside them. An enormous flatscreen TV hung above a gas fireplace. A chest of drawers was positioned beside a walk-in closet. Large windows with a cushioned seat underneath overlooked the river and the eastern range.

He had to admit that everything was modern and well decorated, giving the rustic feeling of being on a ranch without compromising comfort or quality. He understood now—especially after the tour—why the place was so popular.

Braun had followed him up and now strode to the closet, where he'd unpacked Max's clothing and hung everything as neatly as always. While Braun rummaged through the selections, Max pulled off his sweater and his damp socks.

Whenever he was at one of his family's residences, whether the palace in Vollenstadt or the castle up in the mountains or their estate on Bodensee, he always had a valet to assist him with getting dressed. However, during his trips out of the country, he usually only brought his assistant and bodyguard, and he liked a little more independence.

He changed into a casual button-down shirt with a pair of slacks, donned casual loafers, and added a touch of cologne.

"You are certain I do not look overdressed?" He paused at the mirror near the cabin's front door and combed his fingers through his hair.

"You look very presentable." Braun peered over the loft railing from where he was ironing a shirt for Max to wear in the morning.

"Presentable?" Max rubbed his beard. "Should I not be more than presentable?"

"You look handsome, Your Highness."

"You are just saying so to appease me."

"I would never do such a thing."

"Of course not."

Braun tsked, the closest he ever came to laughing.

Max backed away from the mirror. "I do not know why I am so nervous. This is just a casual dinner."

"If it is more than casual, that is okay too, Your Highness."

Would it be okay to have something more than casual with Emberly?

He was well past those days when he'd dated offhandedly and had a new woman every month. He was at a juncture in his life where that lifestyle did not appeal to him anymore, if it ever had.

He most certainly wasn't interested in a weeklong fling with Emberly, and she wouldn't entertain such a notion either. She would likely be strongly against it, which was for the best.

So what was this dinner for?

Her presence was a distraction this week. That was all. It would help him as he tried to gain that perspective she'd mentioned.

At a knock on the door, he blew out a tense breath, ran his fingers through his hair one more time, then opened the door.

Two young men in servers' uniforms stood on the porch with several food warmers between them. "We have your dinner."

Max tried to squelch his disappointment at not seeing Emberly and stepped aside for the young men to enter. The two brought the food into the kitchenette and distributed it onto the table along with setting up the tableware.

They were finishing when the front door opened, and Emberly stepped inside with a bottle of fine wine.

"Welcome." The knot that had been growing tighter inside Max loosened. He approached Emberly and took the wine from her. "I was beginning to wonder if you might change your mind about returning."

"Of course not." She shrugged out of her parka, revealing the clothing she'd worn earlier—a sweatshirt and leggings. Her hair was in the same long braid, and she was still wearing her boots. She clearly hadn't done anything to impress him.

He was most definitely overdressed. He had half a

mind to race up to the loft and change back into the clothing he'd worn earlier too. But he guessed that doing so would only make him look even more foolish.

"I couldn't back out," she said as she hung up her coat. "Not after you worked so hard at asking me politely." Her voice contained a note of humor.

"Good. I appreciate that you are making my efforts worthwhile." As he had when he'd been with her before, he could feel the weight of his responsibilities falling away. There was something about her that was so refreshing and honest and real, that made the other things in his life seem less important. "Perhaps you shall reform me."

"I'm used to making my brothers behave, so it comes naturally to me."

She'd earlier mentioned that she had four brothers and that she was the only girl. As a result, she claimed that she'd grown up as a tomboy, participating in all of the same things they did. She seemed to have a great fondness for her childhood and her brothers, and she still enjoyed fishing and hunting and rock climbing and other activities she'd always done with them.

"So you are considering me one of your brothers, are you?" Max meant the question to be playful. But there was a part of him that didn't want to be relegated to a brother role with Emberly, although it shouldn't matter and was likely for the best.

Emberly was unlacing her boots. "When I told Tyler I was joining you at your cabin for dinner, he wasn't thrilled about the idea."

Max couldn't blame Emberly's brother for his wariness. If the roles had been reversed, Max would have been worried too, especially that some rich guest might be expecting her services to include more than just dinner.

"I told Tyler you had an assistant and a protection agent who would both be at dinner." She slipped off her boots and then straightened, looking Max directly in the eyes. "And I also told my brother you weren't a threat, but that if you did try anything, I would have my knife."

Her knife?

Max almost grinned, but he guessed such a response would not be entirely suitable. Nevertheless, he was strangely pacified that Emberly was not only carrying a knife but threatening to use it on him if necessary. He liked that she was a strong woman who could take care of herself and defend herself from unscrupulous men who might take advantage of her.

"I thank you for the fair warning. I should not wish to lose any of my fingers during dinner."

She held his gaze another moment as though attempting to see inside him and affirm her safety. Even though her eyes were serious, they were big and luminous and beautiful. Framed by long dark lashes, the brown of her eyes was warm and velvety, like a cup of cocoa made by Karltenberg's finest chocolatier.

"Have no fear, Emberly." He gave her what he hoped was a reassuring smile. "You may count me as your newest brother for the week, and I shall regard you as a new sister." Although he'd never had a sister, he had a sister-in-law and knew how to remain friendly with her. He would do the same with Emberly.

"Even so, Tyler will probably send people over to check on me periodically throughout the evening."

"As he should."

The stiffness seemed to ease from Emberly's shoulders.

He was tempted once again to inform her he was a prince and had no need to force himself upon any woman, that he could have a dozen ladies with just a snap of his fingers. In fact, he had a lovely duchess waiting for him to propose marriage—one who was willing to be with him in spite of the awkwardness they experienced with each other.

He swallowed the rising need to defend himself. He would let his character speak for itself.

One thing was certain: Emberly McQuaid was different from any other person he'd ever met. And he liked her that way.

"Rummy!" Emberly placed her run of hearts onto the table.

Winzig tossed his remaining cards down with a grunt. He'd spoken in German to Braun and Max a few times during the evening, but mostly he just grunted.

Across the table from her, Max studied the cards in his hand, then he peered over the edges at her. His brows were furrowed, his eyes serious, and his expression intense. He was competitive and smart and had been challenging to play with, learning the game easily.

Next to Max, Braun paused in knitting a scarf to assess Max's hand. His eyes widened, then he tsked before his needles began clicking again at top speed. A bright-green cashmere scarf was taking shape quickly because, apparently, Braun was an expert knitter.

"Just admit defeat, Max." Emberly couldn't keep from taunting Max the same way she did her brothers. All throughout the evening, she'd done her best to treat Max like a brother, hopefully sending him a clear message that she wasn't interested in being his call girl.

Tyler had been worried that Max was setting her up to be more than just his ambassador. He'd practically yelled at her in her office when she'd told him about going there for a meal tonight. "I'm not letting you have dinner with a stranger in his cabin. You're not his call girl this week."

Tyler had been so opposed to her exclusive arrangement with Max and her plans to eat dinner with him in his cabin that he'd dragged her up to the house in order to gain Dad's support in making her cancel.

Surprisingly, Dad hadn't taken Tyler's side. Instead, he'd studied Emberly's face for a long moment before telling Tyler to let her continue the relationship with Max. At Tyler's exasperation, Dad had finally agreed to the overbearing regulations Tyler had demanded—that ranch employees go regularly to check on Emberly, that she could only be in the cabin if Max's staff remained with him, and that she had to leave no later than ten o'clock.

It was nearing ten, and strangely, she wasn't ready for the evening to come to an end. The whole night from start to finish had been much more enjoyable than she'd expected. Dinner had been relaxed, and Max had regaled her with stories from his childhood in Vollenstadt, which was the capital of Karltenberg. Braun had chimed in with eccentric comments about Max from time to time, which had made both her and Max smile.

After dinner, she'd offered to teach everyone how to play Euchre. Max had known a little from his days in college, but neither Winzig nor Braun had caught on, and eventually she'd decided Rummy would be easier. Winzig had been a good sport and joined in, although he hadn't won a round.

"I cannot admit defeat, Emberly." Max spoke in a voice that mimicked hers. Then he slowly lowered his cards to reveal an even longer run in diamonds—one that put his score into the lead.

She grinned. "Guess I owe you dessert."

"It appears you do." Max grinned in return, his eyes lighting with both playfulness and pleasure. "Double chocolate French silk pie."

They'd decided that whoever won the game owed the other person dessert. It was all in good fun, and she had forgotten to ask the servers to include dessert with their evening meal. So either way, dessert was in order.

"I shall relish every morsel of the pie." Max's voice filled with teasing.

At a knock on the cabin door, she startled. Winzig was up and at the door before she could even move. For a man of his size, he was surprisingly nimble. He was also intimidating, as most protection agents were, including her brother Dustin, who'd been an elite Army Ranger for a number of years before retiring and becoming an executive protection agent.

He now lived in California when he wasn't on assignment, usually out of the country. Whenever he visited the ranch—which had been more often since Dad's diagnosis—he was very close-mouthed about who he was assigned to. Dustin was the quietest of them anyway, and the secrecy of his job made him even more so.

Whatever the case, she understood Winzig's job and wished she could ask him questions about it. But the guy spoke mostly German, and she hadn't yet admitted to everyone that she knew German and could understand them when they switched over to it, which had only been a couple of times.

As Winzig opened the door, he positioned himself so that whoever was on the front porch couldn't see inside very well.

"I'm here to walk Emberly back to her cottage," came her brother Kade's voice.

Emberly stood and quickly crossed to the door. "I don't need anyone to walk me home, Kade."

She knew he wasn't to blame for showing up. Tyler had probably texted him and asked him to come. Even so, she was irritated he was here. The walk to her place in the woods near the lodge was less than a quarter of a mile, and she was used to being out and about the ranch on her own at all times of the day and night.

"Got my orders." Kade tipped up his cowboy hat and angled himself so he could see past Winzig and get a look at Max, who had left the table now too and was crossing to the door.

At twenty-three, Kade was the closest sibling in age to Emberly, and he was also the closest friend among her family. He had a brawny body like the rest of the McQuaid men, all muscle, ruggedly handsome with dark hair and dark eyes. He was slightly taller than the rest of the family, and his face was narrower and more boyish, giving him a charm that made him a favorite among the women for miles around.

Kade spent most of his days as the head of the ranch hands. Though the ranch didn't have a large herd of cattle anymore like in the early days, they still had enough cattle to use as beef for their guests. Mainly, the ranch hands took care of the dozens of horses they bred and raised, and they helped with the weekly rodeos the ranch sponsored during the summer.

"This isn't the military." Emberly couldn't keep the sarcasm from her tone. "And there are no orders. Especially from Tyler."

Kade was still sizing up Max. "Hey."

"Hello." Max stopped by her side, looking professional in his pants and shirt.

She'd tried not to be self-conscious in her comfy clothing, but a part of her regretted that she hadn't taken the time to dress in something nicer. The truth was, she hadn't even considered changing, not until she'd seen Max looking so sleek and polished. Even then, she'd told herself what she wore didn't matter, that she wasn't trying to impress Max or draw his attention.

"I'm just checking on Emberly." Kade spoke calmly while hooking his thumbs through his belt. "Tyler's worried that you're planning to take advantage of her."

"Ka-ade." Emberly's scowl spread. "You can tell Tyler I'm a grown woman and can take care of myself just fine."

Kade shrugged. "Max doesn't look all that threatening. Probably can't wrangle a fly."

"Wrangle a fly?" Max's brow shot up.

"Kade thinks you're weak," Emberly answered bluntly.

"Is that so?" Max drew himself up to his full height, his biceps flexing against his shirt and his shoulders straining at the seams, showing off a body that was definitely not weak.

Max had been a perfect gentleman all evening and hadn't done anything to make her worried about him *taking advantage of her*. In fact, she hadn't noticed anything since she'd met him, other than that he was a little bossy and arrogant at times. But with a prince, she supposed that was to be expected.

Kade grinned at Emberly. "You're trying to get me in trouble."

"Then go on and leave me alone. You shouldn't have come."

"That's what I told Tyler. But he said I had to walk you home."

Emberly appreciated that her brothers cared about her, but sometimes they were overbearing. Especially when it came to the men in her life. They'd scared off plenty of interested guys when she'd been in high school. And the first couple of guys she'd dated in college hadn't lasted long either because of her brothers' pesky interference.

They'd given her a hard time with Ryan too, and he'd complained about them a lot. She'd always wondered whether, if they'd been nicer to him, he would have loved her back.

She doubted it. The truth was, if Ryan had really cared about her enough, he would have loved her regardless of her brothers. But the other part of the truth was that her brothers had a high standard for any man who came into her life.

She would have to make it very clear that Max was just a guest. He wasn't in her life. And there was nothing going on between them except for her being a good hostess and doing her best to make sure Max loved the ranch so that he would go back to his rich friends and talk about it. Word of mouth was everything to marketing, especially a prince's word of mouth.

Was it time to tell her family about Max being a prince? Then maybe they would understand her need to spend time with him and make sure his visit went smoothly. Or maybe they wouldn't understand... Her brothers would probably still be nosy and too protective.

"I know you don't need me along." Kade gave her another one of his irresistible smiles, the kind that made the local girls swoon over him. "But I haven't talked to you in a couple of days. Let me walk you back."

She could sense Max watching her interaction with her brother. Was she holding out hope Max would offer to accompany her home? Surely not. That was ludicrous. Why would he even consider it?

"Fine." She reached for her coat.

Kade chuckled. "Don't act so excited."

"I'll try not to."

Within minutes, she'd said goodbye and was walking with Kade along the shoveled and salted pathway toward the lodge. He was full of questions about Max, and she did her best to be as honest as possible.

Once again, she considered telling him the truth about Max being a prince. But something held her back. Maybe she was afraid that the more people who knew, the easier it would be for someone to slip up and let the word out. Since Max seemed so determined to keep his trip private, the least she could do was protect his secret.

She'd just washed her face and put on her pj's when a knock sounded on the front door of her cottage. The dozen or so employee houses were small but well built, with one bedroom off the great room and kitchen. They were furnished with all modern appliances, supplies, and furniture. The home had been sufficient for her and allowed her to stay close to the staff and the lodge so that she could make herself available for any needs that arose after hours.

After quitting school and returning from Colorado Springs with her tail tucked between her legs, she'd gotten tired of everyone dissecting her life and trying to figure out what had gone wrong and what she should do next. She'd needed to step away and have some breathing space and had moved into an employee cottage.

As much as she loved her family, she liked having her own place, liked taking breaks from her brothers' well-meaning meddling in her life, liked feeling responsible and grown-up, even though her family still treated her like a child sometimes.

She pulled an oversized sweatshirt over her pj's and made her way to the door. As she peeked out the peephole, she drew in a quick breath at the sight of Max standing on her front stoop in the porch light.

She'd left his cabin an hour or so ago. What was he doing here now?

Had Tyler been right to be cautious? Did Max expect more from her?

As soon as that thought came, she shoved it aside. She could read people easily. Max was a good and decent guy. Her time with him today had proven how kind he was.

She opened the door. "Max? Is everything all right?"

He'd had his hands crossed behind his back and now brought them around to reveal a basket. Inside was a French silk pie. She'd called the kitchen as soon as she'd arrived at her cottage and asked them to deliver one to Max. It wasn't a double chocolate, but it was homemade by their pastry chef and was excellent.

His expression was sheepish. "I was hoping you might consider joining me for a piece of pie."

"It's yours. You won it fair and square."

"You deserve it too."

"I couldn't—"

"Please. I would love to have some help eating it."

Winzig stood a dozen paces away in the shadow of another employee cottage.

"I'm sure Winzig would be happy to help you. And Braun—"

"Braun is too busy at the moment with his fantasy football league Zoom call."

"Braun is in a fantasy football league?"

"What you call soccer."

"But Braun?" The expert cashmere-scarf knitter? He

was in a fantasy football—soccer—league?

Max cocked his head. "Are you doubting me?"

"I guess I didn't expect him to have that interest."

"Perhaps people are not always what they seem to be."

Was he referring to himself?

"And Winzig"—Max nodded in the man's direction—"claims he does not like French silk pie."

Emberly released a pretend horrified gasp. "I guess you really do need some help."

He bowed slightly. "I would be greatly honored to have your assistance."

She knew she ought to tell him no. It was getting late, and she was ready for bed. But after being ushered away from his cabin earlier by her brother, she couldn't squelch the frustration that had been festering. She was a twenty-five-year-old woman, for crying out loud. She could decide for herself when to go home for the night. And she could also decide that she wanted to eat pie with a man at 11:00 p.m.

She glanced behind her to her living room with the one sofa. She didn't dare invite Max in. Not only was it against their ranch policy to bring guests into their living quarters, but she didn't let other men—except for family—into her cottage. That had included Ryan when they'd been dating.

Her gaze shifted to the lodge through a thick strand of spruce that hid the employee cottages from the sight of the guests. They could eat at one of the patio tables behind the lodge. But the temperatures had dropped, and they would grow cold too easily.

She could take him up to the dining room. Even though it closed at eleven, she had keys to get in.

She reached for her coat and boots. "Let's go eat pie."

His lips curled up into a slow smile, relaxing his features and making him look more youthful.

As they walked to the lodge, he didn't seem in a hurry and even stopped a couple of times to admire the waterfall in the moonlight. It was especially pretty in the winter, with parts of the cascading water having turned into sheets of ice.

When they reached the dining room, only a few of the staff were still there doing closing tasks. In spite of her bravado, she didn't want word getting back to her brothers about her late-night, pie-eating rendezvous with Max. It wasn't worth their censure. So she detoured into one of the private dining rooms and led him through the dark to a moonlit table near the floor-to-ceiling windows overlooking the river and waterfall.

While Winzig positioned himself outside the door, she and Max sat across from each other with the pie between them and ate right from the dish. He had the thermos of decaf coffee she'd had delivered with the pie, and they sipped coffee out of crystal goblets, the only thing they could find in the room.

The conversation with him flowed easily, as it had the rest of the day. He amused her with pranks he'd pulled during his college years, including letting mice loose in a classroom, tying the president's shirt and pants to a flagpole, and hiding alarm clocks in dorm rooms and having them go off in the middle of the night.

She entertained him with stunts she'd participated in with her brothers while growing up, like the time they'd herded and trapped a bear in the corral, only to have it barrel through the fencing, breaking it into pieces.

When he mentioned a past girlfriend named Sarah, she asked him about his dating life. He admitted to dating lots of women in his younger years, but over recent years, he'd been too busy with work and family responsibilities. He claimed he wasn't in a serious relationship, and when she pressed him for why he wasn't yet married, he offered vague answers that made her realize it was a sensitive topic, one that he didn't want to explain.

In turn, he asked her more about Ryan. She shared about all the things she'd thought they had in common and how they'd seemed like such a perfect fit. Max was such a good listener that she found herself telling him about the McQuaid legacy of love, how the men in her family were lucky because they had inherited the ability to fall in love fast, furious, and forever with a passionate, deep, and enduring love that was totally consuming. Her dad and mom had that kind of love. Tyler had found his legacy love with Kinsey. And Brock had done the same with Venus.

"I admit," she said softly as she leaned back in her chair, "I wish I'd inherited the legacy of love too."

"Perhaps you have."

"No. It's been passed down through the men."

He twisted his empty goblet absently. The pie in the middle was almost half gone, their forks abandoned.

She wasn't sure how long they'd been sitting there. Maybe an hour or more. She hadn't glanced at her phone to check the time, but she guessed it was well past midnight.

"I cannot accept your reasoning, Emberly." Max spoke in a low voice too. "A legacy of love is not a physical trait like eye color. Even if it were, why would the women in the McQuaid family not also have the gene?"

She shrugged. "From the way my dad explains it, the men have always been the ones to go particularly love-crazy over just one woman. He's never mentioned that happening to the McQuaid women."

"Then 'tis possible."

"It didn't happen with me and Ryan."

"Perhaps you have yet to meet the one man who makes you *love-crazy*."

She'd never considered the possibility that she might

have the legacy of love running through her veins. But what if she did?

"Besides," Max continued, "maybe the legacy is something that is passed on more through actions and example than by blood."

"Maybe." She didn't know exactly how the legacy worked. All she knew was that it was something important among the men in her family.

"If your dad saw the way his dad passionately and deeply loved his wife, then he had an example of love to imitate."

"I think you're partly right. But I also believe that some people inherit a more emotional and passionate nature."

"And you did not?"

"I don't think so. Not in the same way as my dad and brothers." She sighed. She'd always wanted to have the kind of marriage her parents had, but she'd despaired of finding someone who would ever measure up to her dad.

Max sat back in his chair and studied her through the moonlight. His eyes were especially dark and brooding at the moment. He opened his mouth to say something, then closed it and pressed his lips together.

"What?" she asked.

"Nothing."

"Just be honest with me, Max. I can take it."

He hesitated. "Very well. I believe you are making an excuse."

"How so?"

"You are resigning yourself to mediocre relationships instead of accepting that relationships will only be—what did you say—as *love-crazy* as you are willing to make them."

Was Max right? Had she resigned herself to a less-than-happy love life? At this point, she still wasn't interested in any love life at all. Even though it had been months since her breakup with Ryan, she had no desire to get involved with anyone else.

"What about you and Sarah?" she asked. "Was that a mediocre relationship?"

He dropped his gaze to his goblet. "My situation is entirely different."

"Oh, so you don't have to work hard to make a relationship work?"

"I have pressures you cannot understand."

"Now who's the one making excuses?"

"No." He pushed back from the table and stood abruptly. "You do not know what you are talking about."

"Explain it."

His body had grown visibly tense and his expression withdrawn. "You have no right to order me to do anything."

"I see. You can lecture me on my relationships, but no one's allowed to do the same to you?"

"I was not lecturing you."

She stood now too, and hugged her arms to her chest. The room had grown colder, but it was his attitude that had decidedly lost its warmth. Should she try to reclaim the camaraderie, perhaps apologize?

But she hadn't done anything wrong—only asked him to be as honest and vulnerable as she'd been with him. Did he think that, because he was a prince, he could require more of her than of himself?

If so, he was mistaken. He might be able to take that superior attitude with his subjects. But she wasn't his subject. She was her own person with her own life and her own needs. She wanted to tell him as much, but in doing so, she would reveal that she knew about his royalty.

"I suppose it is getting late..." Max said as he stepped away from the table.

"Go ahead. Go." She waved at the door. "But just so you know for the future, don't dish out advice that you can't stomach in return." She couldn't stop herself from at least speaking some of the truth.

He paused. Then he nodded before stalking across the room and out the door. She heard him speak tensely with Winzig before his footsteps lightly padded away.

When the hallway door to the stairwell clicked closed, she released a sigh and began to pick up the table, placing the pie, goblets, and thermos back into the basket.

As she started across the room through the darkness, a shadow stepped away from the door, and she let out a gasp. Winzig filled the doorway, and he didn't look happy. "I will walk you home," he said in accented English.

She was tempted to reply in German and tell him to go back to the prince and do his job—which he clearly wanted to do, even though it appeared that Max had ordered him to make sure she made it safely back to her cottage.

She didn't need a protection agent any more than she'd needed Kade earlier. But it was kind of Max to show concern.

Perhaps she had become overly familiar with him. After all, she'd never spent so much time with any one guest before. His leaving so abruptly was a reminder that Max was only visiting the ranch and she was nothing more than his personal concierge. She couldn't forget it. And now that she'd offended him, maybe doing her job would be easier.

6

Max could admit he'd been hoping to encounter Emberly throughout the morning meetings. However, he hadn't glimpsed her once, not even when he'd invented an excuse to walk through the lobby so he could glance past the guest counter and down the hallway toward her office.

"We're heading over to ski." One of the gentlemen near the head of the table pushed back from his chair. "Would you like to join us?"

"I regret that I must decline your invitation." Max stuffed the last folder into his briefcase. "But I shall look forward to hearing about the experience."

Most of the other men had already left the conference room, and as the final few said their farewells to him, he opened his laptop. He had too much work left to do to go skiing.

Besides, he'd recently spent the Christmas holidays skiing in the Alps with his family and so wasn't set on having to ski in Colorado. Although if Emberly was able to plan something private, he would consider going.

Was he terrible for anticipating seeing her again?

Thoughts of her had filled his sleep. Upon waking in the morning, more thoughts of her had flooded his mind, along with the realization that he hadn't ended their time together well the previous night. She hadn't called him a hypocrite, but essentially that's what he'd been. She was right that he'd been doling out counsel for her love life that he was not willing to follow himself.

What was it he had said? Something like *Stop settling for mediocre relationships and start putting in the hard work required to have a good relationship.* He almost laughed at himself now for saying such a thing to Emberly when he had never exerted himself in his relationship with Sarah. No wonder he'd never felt connected to her.

Emberly had been as straightforward as always in pointing out his double standard. Instead of confessing it, he had acted superior and walked away.

No doubt she would want nothing to do with him today, and he would not blame her for that in the least.

With a sigh, he focused on his laptop, clicked onto the tab with his emails, and opened the most urgent of the dozen or more that had come in over the morning. It should be of no consequence what Emberly thought of him or that she might not spend any more time with him. But strangely, it did matter.

He was trying to understand why he cared so much about seeing her, why he felt a longing to be with her and talk with her and spend time with her. He had just met her, hardly knew her, and would never see her again once he left.

Regardless, the need inside had been building in his chest all morning. Did the need have to do with how beautiful she was? He wanted to get his fill of her exquisite features, striking red hair, and warm eyes again today and see if she was truly as gorgeous as he remembered.

Or did the need have to do with how much fun he'd had with her doing ordinary things like hiking, eating dinner, playing cards, and eating pie? She was comfortable to be with, unpretentious, and he felt as though he could be himself—or at least the part of himself that wasn't royalty.

The truth was, Emberly was a refreshing change from every woman he'd ever known, and the craving to be with her was only growing. The other truth was that he'd neglected his work for most of yesterday. Of course, he'd worked late into the night, and today he had been doing his best to concentrate on his tasks. It would not be the end of the world if she chose to ignore him. Or assign him a new concierge.

She would not do that, would she?

He sat up and stared through the glass walls to the

hallway that led to the lobby. Perhaps that was why she was not around. Perhaps she was even now making the arrangements with another concierge.

With his heart suddenly thudding faster, he pushed back and stood. He had to stop her from leaving with one of the other groups and insist that she remain with him instead.

No, he could not insist. That would be rude of him. He would have to use his best manners and implore her politely.

He stuffed his laptop into his briefcase, gathered up a few scattered notes, then quickly exited the conference room.

Winzig, who had been waiting in the hallway, trailed him to the lobby. Max had no intention of simply walking past the offices this time. He would go right in and find her and talk to her. And apologize. Yes, he would also apologize for his callousness the previous night.

As he started across the lobby, he caught sight of first her red hair and then her profile as she stood near the long counter and spoke to what appeared to be guests—a young couple. He wanted to go right over, interrupt the conversation, and tell her to drop everything in order to be with him. But he slowed his steps and halted a few feet away.

She did not spare him a glance. Did she not notice his

presence? How could she not?

Max hesitated. Most places he went, people catered to his every whim and wish. They flattered and groveled before him.

Had he grown so accustomed to preferential treatment that he had become arrogant, impatient, and entitled? It would seem her honesty was helping him to reflect on areas in his life that needed to be addressed. Associating with her was quite possibly turning him into a better man. One who would be well equipped to lead a nation—if he didn't abdicate to Alex.

Emberly spoke for a few more moments, then smiled at the couple as they thanked her and walked away. Only when they were near the door did she allow herself to shift and look at him.

Max half expected her to notice him, then turn on her heels and stalk away. But she didn't move. Instead, she watched him almost expectantly, as if she were waiting for him to speak first.

"I owe you an apology." The words fell out and felt right. "I regret suggesting something for you that I was not willing to demand of myself."

"Apology accepted." She did not smile, but the brown of her eyes was warm, and her expression held no trace of malice.

"Thank you." He was not used to such freely given forgiveness.

"How were your meetings this morning?" she asked politely.

As with yesterday when he had first encountered her, she was attired in a professional skirt, a blouse trimmed with lace, and a form-fitting blazer. Her hair was again styled into the elegant knot, drawing attention to her slender neck, and her ears were dainty and graced with simple pearl earrings.

"The meetings were rushed because, of course, the men were eager to partake in skiing and other activities."

"Are you eager too?"

"Perhaps." He was eager to be with her. But he could not say so. "What outings do you have for us this afternoon? You are still planning on leading the activities, are you not?" He hoped he did not sound too pathetic, because that was how he was starting to feel regarding this woman.

One of her brows quirked adorably. "Were you worried I wouldn't do my job today?"

"I confess, I was worried I might have tried your patience and that you would be ready to be rid of me."

"You have tried my patience." Her lips curled up into a slight smile. "But I'm a woman of my word, and you can't scare me away that easily."

"Good." Relief rushed through him. "When will you be available to begin our activities?"

"Whenever you are."

"I am free now."

What was he saying? He had to attend to the issues that had arisen during the meetings, another new, important client, and a dozen other items on his itinerary. He needed to find a quiet place to work for at least several more hours. But he couldn't make himself say it, because the truth was, he wanted to spend time with her.

"What would you like to try first?" She pointed to a poster on the wall behind the desk that had large, colorful photos of people engaging in various activities.

He didn't bother to examine them closely, because he honestly didn't care what he did as long as he was with her. "What do you suggest?"

"Based on what I've learned about you, I think you would enjoy the cross-country skiing, snowshoeing, or the downhill skiing."

"Correct. I have done them all and enjoy them. But I should like you to introduce me to something different, something I may not have accomplished before."

Her smile quirked up on one side, making her look mischievous in a completely enticing way. "Would you like me to show you my favorite?"

"I would be delighted to discover your favorite." For a reason he could not explain, he truly meant the words. He wanted to learn more about her, what she enjoyed, what she was good at, and what she did for entertainment.

"How about if we change into warmer clothing and meet back here at the front of the lodge in an hour?"

"What will we be doing?"

"You'll have to wait. It's a surprise."

Without giving him the opportunity to respond, she made her way around the counter and down the hallway toward her office.

Surprise? *She* was a surprise, doing things he was not expecting, things most people simply did not do with a prince, like telling him he'd have to wait for a surprise. Had he ever been surprised in his life?

He could do nothing less than stare after her as she walked away in her heels, her hips swaying just enough to draw his attention to her body and all her lovely curves. She looked as fantastic today in her professional attire as she had last night in her casual clothing. Truthfully, he could not imagine a time when Emberly, as naturally beautiful as she was, would ever look anything other than stunning.

Before she entered her office, she paused and glanced back at him with a lift of her brow, as though she'd felt his stare following her.

Perhaps an ordinary man would have felt embarrassed for staring so blatantly. But he was accustomed to staring as openly as he wanted and at whatever he wanted. She was meant to be admired. He was committing no crime in simply doing the required duty.

She just shook her head slightly before stepping into her office and closing her door.

Once she was out of sight, he stared a moment longer, then forced himself to disengage. He wasn't sure what was going on inside him, but he was starting to feel somewhat smitten with Emberly McQuaid. And smitten wasn't the emotion he needed to facilitate with her.

He returned to his cabin, where Braun was polishing Max's leather dress shoes while blaring an audiobook on the Reformation and the invention of the printing press. Braun paused the monologue to assist Max into a casual outfit of faded jeans and a corduroy shirt.

With his stomach growling, Max had Braun track down Emberly's phone number and text her about meeting him for lunch. She agreed and offered to arrange a secluded table in the loft of the Brook Barn.

"You can text me yourself, you know," she said as she took the spot across from him at the table in the loft. Only one other couple dined on the opposite side of the quiet and cozy area that overlooked the main floor of the restaurant.

"I did not wish to impose upon you." He picked up the menu at his place.

She snorted. "And Braun's texts aren't imposing?"

"I suppose they are too. I apologize—"

"Max." Her voice was firm, but her eyes were gentle.

"You don't need to keep apologizing for everything."

"I would rather be overly remorseful than not care enough."

She paused and seemed to search his face before nodding. "You're a good man, Max."

"It's kind of you to say so." If only he felt good enough lately, but the fact was that he had felt lacking for quite some time.

"Give me your phone." She held out her hand.

He hesitated. Did he have any identifying information there that would reveal his princely status? He didn't want to disclose it to her yet, not with how much he was enjoying himself in this unusual position of not being known.

He swiped up and quickly scanned his screen. As far as he could tell, he didn't have anything overtly revealing.

He handed it to her.

She took it, put her private phone number into his contacts, and handed it back. Then she typed something on her phone. A few seconds later a text dinged.

He read the new message that had popped up.

Emberly: *Thank you for your honesty last night.*

She was busy studying her menu—or at least pretending to.

Not only was Emberly incredible, but she was clearly humble enough to accept feedback. That was a rare quality indeed—one he truly admired in people. He typed out a message of his own.

Max: *I appreciate your honesty in return.*

She glanced at her phone, then began working on another message.

His stomach fluttered with something strange. Was it the butterflies so many talked about? Was this woman giving him butterflies? If so, that was a first.

Her text came through a second later.

Emberly: *I'm going to work hard for a love-crazy relationship.*

She was? With whom? He wanted to ask if she had anyone in mind. Perhaps he would later. However, for now, he needed to keep that question to himself or risk coming across as too intrusive.

Max: *I shall do likewise. Love-crazy all the way.*

As she read his reply, she smiled. She set down her phone, pushed it aside, then met his gaze. "It's worth a try, isn't it?"

"I agree."

He wanted to say more, although he wasn't sure what, but a server approached to take their order, and after that, the conversation moved to other topics. Even so, his mind kept repeating his text. *Love-crazy all the way.*

He'd essentially vowed to Emberly that he would work hard at a love relationship. Did that mean he needed to get back together with Sarah and put forth more effort, or should he seek out someone new in the two remaining months until his birthday?

Either way, he had to work hard at having a love-crazy relationship. He didn't know if it was possible to have one. But he did know he had to try.

7

Was she enjoying her time with Max too much?

Emberly's shot easily hit the clay disk that had been tossed in the air to imitate a bird. She lowered her Browning shotgun and grinned at Max, who stood beside her in the shooting stand.

"I can see why clay shooting is your favorite activity." Max was holding his shotgun and staring at the clay tile now cracked on the ground. Most of the snow from yesterday had melted away under the high-altitude sun, leaving only a few patches behind in the shade. The clumps of grass were yellowed and damp. The sagebrush was brown and scraggly. And the prairie dog hills were lonely and lifeless.

Regardless of how bedraggled it looked, the grassland was peaceful. It was in a secluded part of the ranch away from the rest of the activities, lodging, and guests so that no one would inadvertently get caught in the crossfire. In fact, they'd used an ATV to reach the shooting range with its modern array of equipment, targets, and guns. The spacious cabin behind them contained the instructors' offices as well as a coffee bar and snacks, along with comfortable seating for the guests. The overhang above the wide structure and the outdoor wood-burning stove allowed practice in all sorts of weather, even throughout the winter.

"Don't feel too bad," she teased. "We can't all be good at everything."

"Oh, prideful much?" Through the thick lens of his protective gear, his eyes sparkled with playfulness.

"When it comes to this ranch? Yes." She loved the easy way she could banter with Max, similar to how she bantered with her brothers.

"You have beaten me at both trap and skeet shooting. So I suppose I ought to give credit where credit is due."

"Yes, you should."

He removed the protective glasses and perched them on top of his head. "When you come to Karltenberg, I shall challenge you to the European way of clay shooting."

"When I come to Karltenberg?"

He took off his noise-blocking earmuffs. "Perhaps you will come someday, and I can return the favor of taking you around to my favorite activities."

She slipped off her glasses and earmuffs too. Was Max

being serious, or was he only being nice? And what did it really matter?

This morning when she'd arrived at her office, she hadn't been able to resist googling him. A whole host of pictures had flooded her laptop screen, of him with various women—movie stars, other royalty, models, and more. All of them had been beautiful and rich and famous.

Then there had been the pictures of him with Sarah, who, as it turned out, happened to be the Duchess of Bavaria. She, too, was pretty and nearly perfect in every way. From all accounts, Sarah had been devastated to lose Max, especially because she'd hoped for a proposal, and instead, he'd delivered a breakup. If he went back home and worked harder at his relationship with her, no doubt he could make things work.

Even though last night's discussion about relationships had made him uncomfortable, she wasn't ready to let the topic go quite yet. "What will your wife think of you inviting me to come visit and taking me around to all your favorite activities?"

"My wife?" Max set aside his gun and supplies. "I thought you knew I am single."

"You won't be forever."

He bent and retrieved a log from the woodpile, opened the stove door, and added more fuel. As he straightened, he expelled a tight breath. "I suppose if I implement our agreement to work hard in a relationship, I shall hopefully facilitate love."

"You're a great guy, Max. I'm sure women have an easy time falling in love with you."

"Easy time falling in love, eh? I assume you are referencing yourself in the matter."

"Oh, you guessed it," she deadpanned. "It was love at first sight."

"Precisely what I expected."

This time she rolled her eyes.

He chuckled.

"If women fall in love with you so quickly, then I guess that means you're the one not falling in love back."

His mirth faded, and the muscles in his jaw ticked.

Was she pushing him too much? If only she could control her curiosity. "Why haven't you fallen in love with anyone yet?"

He paced back to the railing of the shooting stand and peered out over the barren landscape.

She surveyed the land too. The wide-open range with its thick grass had drawn her relatives to begin ranching cattle so long ago. And it had drawn lots of McQuaids ever since. It was easy to love the land and the mountains and the beauty of it all. And she did . . .

But there were times when she felt stuck, when she couldn't help wondering if her life would have turned out differently if she hadn't failed out of school, if she'd kept going with her degree in business. Where would she be now? Would she have made a life for herself apart from her family?

Shoulders slumping, Max stuffed his hands in his pockets. "I was in love once. Long ago."

The hollowness in his voice tugged at Emberly. She crossed to the railing and stood beside him. She might not be able to say or do anything to take that hollowness and hurt away, but at least she could listen.

"Ava. She was my tutor's daughter." His tone dropped low. "She came to the tutoring sessions with Mr. Koch, her father, and we became good friends."

"How old were you?"

"Sixteen when I first met her, and naturally, our friendship turned into more. She was my first kiss, first love, first everything."

"Sounds like you really cared for her."

He was silent for a heartbeat. "Before I left for Cambridge, I gave her a promise ring and asked her to wait for me."

Emberly could guess the direction of his story, and already her heart ached for him.

"The first year I was gone, she met and married someone else."

The first year? That was fast. And to marry someone else? That was brutal. "That's really crummy. I'm sorry, Max."

He didn't say anything for a long moment. "It shattered me, and I coped the only way I knew how. I attempted to drown out the pain and forget about her."

"I guess that didn't work so well, huh?"

He shrugged. "It worked well enough."

"You obviously haven't forgotten about her and are still hurt by her betrayal."

"I have forgiven her," he said sadly. "But I have not forgiven her father for accepting the bribe from my father to marry her off as quickly as possible."

"Oh wow. That's terrible."

"What my father did was unforgivable too. But he has always been more rigid about... well, about the protocols in my family. But Mr. Koch? I thought he was open-minded and did not abide by old customs and class differences."

The ache inside Emberly swelled, and before she could stop herself, she laid a hand on Max's arm.

He didn't brush her aside, but neither did he acknowledge her touch. He continued to stare straight ahead, his jaw taut.

No wonder Max was still single. He'd fallen in love once and had never really gotten over all that had happened. "Max," she started slowly. "You obviously want to move on from this, otherwise you wouldn't have promised me that you would work hard at a love-crazy relationship."

He remained rigid, as though he might spin and walk away. But after a moment, he released a breath and nodded. "I have tried to move beyond what happened. Many times. But perhaps I am doomed to be haunted by it forever."

"You're not doomed. But you are stuck, and maybe you need a little push to de-stick you."

"De-stick?" He slanted a glance her way. "If that is a word, I am not familiar with it."

"Fine." She dropped her hand away from him. "It's not a word. But that's not the point."

"What is your point?"

"You need someone to help you see your potential to love again."

He shifted so that now he was facing her, leaning his hip against the railing. "Would that someone happen to be you?"

"Maybe."

"So you are not only the ranch expert, but you are also the expert in matchmaking?"

"I'm no expert, and I'm no matchmaker. But I have learned a lot about the McQuaid legacy of love through watching my dad and brothers—enough that I can give you a few tips on how to win over a woman."

"You are suggesting that would help?"

"If you want to know how to love a woman well, then there's no better person to learn from than a McQuaid, especially my dad."

"I have no wish to disturb your father with this matter."

"We won't. I'm just saying that he's a wise person, and there's a lot to be learned from looking at the way he did things."

Max nodded. "Very well. If you wish to instruct me on how to win and love a woman, then I shall do my best to humbly receive the advice."

A winter breeze blew against Emberly and through her parka. She shuddered. "First word of advice: Always, always be paying attention to the woman's needs. For example, when she's cold, you really need to notice." This time she shivered on purpose.

His eyes lit up with humor. "I see how this arrangement is going to work. You will expect me to practice your advice on you."

"You know what they say. Practice makes perfect."

"Agreed. So once I notice the woman is cold, what shall I do first?"

"You'll do everything within your power to make sure she warms up and is comfortable."

"Shall I give you my coat?"

"That's one possibility."

He began unzipping his heavy jacket.

She halted him halfway with her mittened hand. "In this instance, you should keep your coat. Instead, you should pull me closer—"

She wasn't able to finish her sentence before he was tugging her under his jacket. He drew her gently against his side and wrapped one arm around her, situating her as carefully as if she were made of glass.

"How is that?" he asked. "Warmer?"

She was trying hard not to think about the fact that she was pressed up against Max. "I was saying you could pull me closer *to the stove*, but this does the trick too."

He shuffled forward toward the stove, bringing her with him and not releasing her. As soon as they were positioned in front of the blazing fire, he tucked her more securely in the crook of his body, as though he had no intention of letting go.

She didn't resist. Because of the warmth of his hold. That was all. "You're passing your first test with high marks."

"I always strive to do my best."

She smiled and leaned her head against him. Even if this was all pretend, she was here for it. It had been too long since she'd had a man hold her so tenderly. Had Ryan ever really been tender with her? Not in their last months together, that was for sure. He'd been cold and distant, and she should have seen the end coming. So why hadn't she?

Had she set her standards too low for Ryan? Had she figured that since she was a woman, she could never expect the kind of love or marriage her parents had? Maybe in believing the McQuaid legacy of love could never be hers, she'd settled for less. Was it time to expect more? To not settle for anything less than a love-crazy man?

"You have grown quiet," Max stated softly. "What are you thinking about?"

"Ryan."

"Do I remind you of him?" The question was hesitant.

"Not at all. You're very different."

"So why think of him now?"

"I was just realizing Ryan was never really all that crazy about me."

Max's arm flexed against her as though he was tightening his hold. "He clearly was a fool for giving you up."

"A fool, huh?" She knew the breakup hadn't been entirely Ryan's fault, that it took two people to make a relationship succeed or fail. She obviously had her faults too. But it was nice to hear Max's defense.

"Yes, you are beautiful and smart . . . and you know how to shoot a gun better than most men."

She laughed lightly, pleasure awakening inside her at his compliment. High praise, coming from a man who'd dated such an elite lineup of women over the years. "Since it appears that you're able to dole out compliments, we can check that off your to-do list in winning a woman over."

"I am quite good at the charm when I put my mind to it."

"The compliments have to be genuine."

"Are you worried about my being truthful? If so, you need not, as I have never been more sincere." His voice turned low and earnest. "You truly are stunning in every way."

"Thank you, Max." The pleasure inside her swelled.

"I am just stating the obvious."

She caught a whiff of his cologne, as she had on a few other occasions—a rich, woodsy scent of mahogany, likely from a brand that cost more than she made in a week. She had the urge to lean into him and breathe more deeply of him, but she knew she had to be careful not to get carried away with this pretending.

She shouldn't take him so seriously, shouldn't allow herself to care about what he thought, shouldn't even be standing so close to him. It wasn't appropriate for her to do so with a guest.

As the thought jabbed her, the cabin door opened and one of the range instructors stepped out onto the porch. He had his arms filled with gear and pretended not to see her, but it was obvious he had already noticed her in the much-too-intimate position with Max.

"We were just finishing." She tugged away from Max

and straightened her spine.

Max didn't move. Instead, he held himself with a bearing that seemed to claim his right to be there doing whatever he wanted regardless of what anyone thought of him.

She didn't have that luxury. She had to care. The ranch's reputation depended on it.

"Didn't mean to rush you, Miss McQuaid," the young man said, still not looking in her direction. "But a group is pulling up."

"Of course." She was surprised at how much she'd enjoyed her time with Max. Even so, she couldn't forget she was doing a job, and that's all this was for both of them.

As she idled the ATV in front of his cabin a short while later, the late-afternoon shadows were long, and the sky was already losing its brilliance. "Have a good night, Max."

He didn't make a move to leave. Instead, he stared straight ahead at the cabin. His profile was angular and lean, and the short layer of beard only added to his appeal.

When he turned his gaze upon her, his eyes were intense. "Come in and have dinner with me again tonight."

She started to shake her head.

"I would love your company."

"You've had my company all afternoon."

"It went by too fast."

It had gone by fast for her too, but she couldn't admit that. "I thought you had work to do."

"It can wait."

She hesitated.

"Please, Emberly?" The earnestness in his tone and eyes was too hard to resist.

Besides, she didn't really want to resist, even though she knew she should. With her indiscretion at the shooting range, she'd likely only added fuel to the gossip about her and Max. No doubt her brothers would hear and would scold her later.

Max reached across and touched her arm with his gloved hand. "Would it help if I beg?"

She loved that he was willing to beg her to spend time with him. Not many men would be humble enough to do it at the risk of coming across as pathetic. But he was far from pathetic. Everything about him was instead magnetic.

"Fine, Max." She pretended exasperation as she lifted his hand away from her arm. "But you have to agree that there won't be any more physical contact, not even innocently."

"Agreed." He wedged his hands into his coat pockets.

"And no flirting."

"Agreed again."

"Then okay. I'll be back in an hour."

He smiled. "You have made my night."

"I find that difficult to believe."

"'Tis true."

"I'm sure you've had much more fun than I can offer."

"Do not be too sure about that."

She wanted to blurt out in that moment that she knew he was a prince and that his life was much more exciting than hers. But a burly figure walking toward them halted her words.

It was Tyler, and his face was tight with anger. "I'm assigning Max a new ambassador."

Emberly had half a mind to squeal the ATV and ride away and ignore Tyler. But Max didn't move, and she couldn't ride away with him by her side.

Instead, she sat up straighter and faced her brother. "I'm in charge of the ambassadors, not you."

"I just got word that you were seen cozying up with him." Tyler stopped in front of the ATV and waved a hand between her and Max. "You're done with whatever this is."

"Relax." She had known Tyler would hear about the incident. She just hadn't expected the gossip to fly so fast. "There's nothing going on."

"It doesn't sound like that to me."

She pinched the bridge of her nose and tried to find

the appropriate response.

Before she could, Max was stepping out of the ATV. His expression had hardened. "Your insinuations are not only inappropriate, they are also disrespectful of Emberly."

Tyler shifted his glare onto Max. "You're the one being inappropriate and disrespectful."

"That is not my intention at all."

"Then leave Emberly alone."

"Tyler." She spoke firmly as her frustration began to mount. "I am Max's ambassador for his stay here at the ranch, and you can't track me down every time you hear a rumor."

"I'm in charge of the ranch—"

"Then let me do my job."

Tyler opened his mouth to protest, but his phone began ringing. He glanced at it, then shot Max another glare. "If I find out you're not treating my sister respectfully, you'll wish you never came here." With that, he spun and stalked away while taking the phone call.

Emberly stared after him, her resolve to spend time with Max growing, if only to show Tyler that he couldn't interfere like this.

Max sighed. "I apologize for causing the strife—"

"Dinner in an hour?" Emberly asked.

Max's brows rose. "You are certain?"

"More than certain." In fact, she planned to spend as

much time with Max as she wanted without letting her meddling family interfere. "Whatever you want to do, I'm here for you."

8

The last four days at the ranch had passed much too quickly. Max couldn't believe he had only one day left. He and the other gentlemen were driving to Denver tomorrow to catch their flight home.

He glanced at his laptop and the email he was composing and tried not to sigh with impatience. But he let out a breath anyway.

At the cabin table across from him, Braun glanced up from examining several new stamps he had discovered yesterday at an antique store in Healing Springs. With the loupe in one eye, he examined Max instead.

"She should be here by now." He didn't owe Braun an explanation, but he felt as though he should give one nonetheless.

"Would you like me to phone her, Your Highness, and let her know you are waiting?"

"Not at all." Such a call would never work with

Emberly. And the truth was, he was merely being impatient.

But who could blame him? The previous days with her had been nothing short of amazing. *She* was amazing. Each day, after his morning meetings with the board members, he had met her in the lobby just as he had the first day. They'd had lunch together in their private corner of the loft in the Brook Barn. Then they'd spent one afternoon ice fishing, one day cross-country skiing, and another downhill skiing.

They'd had dinner together every night in his cabin with Winzig and Braun. Afterward, they'd played cards or other games, then ended their night with a gourmet dessert in secret in the banquet room overlooking the waterfall, sometimes talking for several more hours before finally going back to their respective cabins and catching a few hours of sleep.

His work had suffered, to be sure. He hadn't been able to keep up with everything, only the most urgent. However, the further the week had progressed, the more he'd realized that nothing was truly urgent. He had also realized his assistants in the bank in Vollenstadt were more capable of handling the details than he'd supposed.

Throughout the week, he'd finally let go of the frustrations that had been plaguing him. He wasn't sure if it had been cutting back on his work or being on the ranch or participating in the activities that had played a role in making him feel less burdened. Perhaps being around Emberly had impacted him. Whatever the case, he could gradually feel himself gaining a perspective on life again. He still wasn't sure what he would do when he returned to Karltenberg, but he wasn't as stressed about it.

He'd appreciated that Emberly made everything as private as possible, and the board members had done well in honoring his request for anonymity. As a result, there had been no sign of the paparazzi.

Her brothers Tyler and Kade, however, often randomly showed up during the activities, which told Max they were keenly aware of all Emberly was doing and were keeping a watchful eye on her, much to her irritation. But in spite of their nosiness, she'd continued to spend time with him.

Hopefully, Max had proven to her brothers he did not have ulterior motives with Emberly. He'd had plenty of opportunities to let their relationship turn into something more intimate, especially because they had been engaging one another more familiarly all week with her so-called lessons on how to win a woman, although none involved touching.

He'd respected her wishes to maintain appropriate physical boundaries after the incident at the shooting range. He could admit he'd loved the feel of her so close and had enjoyed holding her much more than he should have. And he could admit he'd thought about holding her again. His attraction to her was very real, and he couldn't deny it, even if he didn't give in to it.

He had definitely learned a great deal from her—from her dad's wisdom. As she'd shared the ways to win a woman, their exchanges had been all in good fun. Much of her advice had been simple and full of common sense, like asking good questions, showing undivided interest, expressing tenderness, and putting the other's needs first.

For his last day on the ranch, he'd hoped to have a full day with her. However, she had texted that she would meet him at his cabin after one o'clock. She had offered no explanation for where she was or what she was doing, and now it was close to one thirty with no word from her.

The truth was, he was not feeling impatient because he was anxious to begin the activities of the day. No, he was feeling impatient because he did not want to waste a single minute of the time he had left with her. It honestly had not mattered what they were doing. Being with her was all he'd cared about.

At a rapping on the door, he pushed back his laptop and stood. The soft but determined knock belonged to Emberly. Was he pitiful for already recognizing something so insignificant about her? Perhaps. But he did not care.

As usual, she didn't wait for anyone to answer, instead opening the door and letting herself in. She had her parka on over her casual after-work clothing—leggings and a sweatshirt. He loved the way the leggings showcased her legs, made them look endless, as if his legs could get lost tangling with hers.

Tangling legs? What was he thinking? He couldn't let his thoughts go that direction. And he couldn't dwell on the heat that was spearing his gut.

"Are you ready to figure out the activity of the afternoon?" She took off her hat, and her hair spilled over her shoulders and down her back—long, thick waves that gleamed in the sunlight slanting through the window, the red a warm and inviting color that seemed to beckon to him.

He wanted to cross to her, dig his fingers into her hair and then bend close and breathe her in, maybe even bury his face against her hair. Was he crazy for wanting to do that?

Yes, he was clearly obsessing over her at the moment and needed to stop.

"Max," she gently chided, her brow furrowing. "I think we need to do a quick love-crazy lesson here."

"We do?" His question came out sounding as though he had no brain. He cleared his throat. "Of course. What do you have in mind?"

"You could use some practice on how to interact when a woman first steps into a room."

"Acting like a buffoon is not acceptable?" He tried for a teasing voice.

She finally offered him a smile, but it only made her all the more beautiful, so that he wanted to keep staring at her.

"If you want to make her feel special, then say or do something that tells her you really notice her and care that she's there."

"What do you have in mind?"

"If you're busy with work or watching TV or on your phone, you have to pause whatever you're doing. That's the first step."

"I can do that."

"Good. You're a fast learner," she bantered. "Now think of a way to communicate that you care about her. You sit back down and pretend to work. I'll go back outside, and when I come in, show me."

She didn't give him time to respond. Instead, she opened the door and stepped out, shutting the door behind her.

Max stared at the spot for a moment, then dropped into his chair and drew his laptop back in front of him.

From the corner of his eyes, he could see Braun staring at him with his loupe still in his eye. The interaction with Emberly would likely be the afternoon entertainment, but Max could not protest now. Not with Emberly already opening the door.

As she stepped back inside, Max pretended to be busy for a second. Then he made a point of looking directly at her. "Good afternoon. You look pretty this afternoon."

She shook her head. "Too fast. Take your time and give her a smoldering look, one that really tells her you're checking her out."

She went out again. They practiced a few more times, first with him complimenting her, then winking, and finally whispering an endearment.

"I'm going to act like something is wrong this time," she said as she stepped into the cabin again. "As I walk in, you have to show concern."

She threw off her parka and then started toward the refrigerator with heavy steps.

He pretended to work as he had the past few times, and as she drew near, he glanced away from his laptop and acknowledged her presence.

Her lashes were low, and her lips puckered in a pout.

He wanted to smile at how adorable she looked, but he would only earn her ire if he did so. Instead, he latched onto her arm. "Come here."

As she halted in front of him, she fisted a hand and started to lower it to her hip.

He reached her hip first and tugged her down, surprising himself by guiding her to his lap. What was he doing? He was breaking their no-contact agreement, and he should stand right back up and apologize.

But she didn't resist and perched on the edge of his legs, obviously thinking he was still in his usual mode as a pupil.

Little did she know that learning from her was suddenly the furthest thing from his mind. All he could think about was that she was soft and warm and smelled of sunshine and citrus. He slipped his arm around her, drew her closer, and leaned his head against hers.

She stilled. "Good. This is very good."

At the feel of her backside on his thighs and her curves brushing his chest, the heat inside him sparked into a full fire. Pulling her down onto his lap probably had not been his finest idea.

"Ask me what's wrong," she whispered.

"What is wrong?" He rubbed his fingers across her back, skimming long strands and trying not to let his hands slide higher into her hair. If he did that, he would surely lose his sanity. And he would most definitely be taking this lesson too far.

"Your question would be even better if you used a sweet name. My dad says *darlin'*."

"Darling."

"No, say the whole thing again."

"What is wrong, darling?" His voice came out almost gruff.

"Oooh, perfect," she crooned in his ear. She didn't move away, and instead, her breathing filled his senses.

His own breathing turned shallow and rapid. He longed to pull her back further. Maybe even kiss her.

Kiss her. The longing to do so swelled within him

swiftly. He could only imagine how she would kiss. This was Emberly, and she would likely approach kissing the way she did everything else—boldly and passionately and eagerly.

He couldn't think about it. But it was too late. The fire inside him began to spread, charging through his body so that he wanted to kiss her more than anything else. It was almost as if kissing her was the only thing that could quench the heat inside him.

At a loud throat-clearing nearby, Emberly jumped. At her momentum, he had no choice but to release her.

She scrambled to her feet, her eyes wide and bright and her cheeks flushed. She pressed her hands against her chest as though trying to still her heartbeat. Before he could say anything, she stalked to the door and retrieved her coat.

Was her pulse racing as hard as his was? He was tempted to flatten his hand against his chest too, but he crossed his arms instead, trying to steady himself.

Braun turned the page of his stamp collection book and began to hum a soft tune. His expression was filled with innocence, as if he didn't have a care in the world and had not just witnessed Max sharing a heated moment with Emberly.

It had been heated. Max could not deny it. Neither could he deny that his desire for her was becoming difficult to resist. He had liked her from the start, and his admiration of her had only grown during the week, with the endless hours talking and teasing and enjoying her company.

Yes, he was most certainly attracted to this beautiful and engaging woman. If he was honest, he had not experienced this level of attraction to a woman in a very long time, maybe even since Ava.

So what was he to do about his feelings? Especially since he had just this one day remaining?

A part of him wanted to throw caution aside and let the day unfold as it would. If he ended up kissing Emberly at some point, what was the harm in that? She seemed to be drawn to him as well. Perhaps they could have a goodbye kiss as a way to remember each other.

Max inwardly sighed. No. He could not allow it of himself. He had assured her he had no ulterior motives in having her help this past week, and he intended to be a man of his word. He would never want to give her even the slightest doubt about his honor.

Braun's interruption had been well-timed and just what Max needed. He could not let himself get carried away with this beautiful American woman. Not now on the final day, and not after he had already resisted all week. He couldn't let down his resolve at the last hour.

For the rest of his visit, he had to make sure he did not put them in any more compromising situations where he might be tempted to act upon his feelings for her. He had to keep his focus on being friends. Friendship with this incredible woman had to suffice.

That meant he also had to put an end to these flirtatious lessons. He couldn't pretend any longer that he was thinking about another woman, particularly Sarah, every time Emberly gave him advice on how to be more affectionate and in love.

Because the truth was, during his lessons, the only woman that filled his mind was Emberly. He wanted to win *her* over with all her lessons, wanted to do everything authentically, wanted their time together to be real.

But that was not possible, was it? They lived half a world apart, and they had completely divergent lives. He could not give up everything to be with her, and he certainly would never expect her to give up everything to be with him. He also could not fathom having a long-distance relationship, not with how busy they both were.

Besides, she had never once hinted at wanting a relationship with him. He was arrogant for even thinking she might. In fact, she might be disappointed in him for hiding his true identity from her this past week, for deceiving her into thinking he was an average man. He had considered telling her a time or two early in the week, but mostly he'd forgotten it was even an issue.

The best thing was to stay firm in his decision to appreciate and enjoy her company while it lasted. Then he would return to his life in Karltenberg and finally make the difficult choice between abdicating his right to the throne or accepting and working on the arranged marriage with Sarah.

9

Perched on the split-rail fence on one side of the rodeo arena, Max tucked his new cowboy boots under the rail and watched as Emberly showed off her skills at breakaway roping.

The grandstands and the VIP boxes of the outdoor arena were empty. The bullpens and holding area were dark and deserted. Only a few stadium lights were on to highlight their makeshift rodeo, and they highlighted her in all her beauty.

With a rope in one hand and the reins in the other, she sat in the saddle of her American quarter horse, a stocky chestnut named Princess, that Emberly said she'd had since she was a teenager.

As Kade released the latch on the pen beside her, a bleating calf scurried out. In the next instant, Emberly began the chase, moving quickly and nimbly. At the same time, she skillfully twirled her lasso above her head and then tossed it and looped it around the calf's neck. As soon as the ring was tight enough that it couldn't come off, Emberly released her hold on the rope and let the calf go.

Kade gave a whoop from where he was sitting on the top post of the calf pen. "Eight and a half seconds!"

Emberly reined Princess to an abrupt halt, then tipped up the brim of her tan cowboy hat. She wore a pair of well-worn blue jeans, a thick wool flannel shirt, and cowboy boots. The outfit looked good on her. So good Max couldn't stop admiring the curve of her long legs and hips and waist, even though he knew he should not.

"You sure you don't want to join me on the rodeo circuit?" Kade asked with a grin for his sister. "You've still got what it takes."

Emberly veered Princess around and flashed a smile at Kade. The smile was wide and happy and full of life. The sight of it made Max's chest tighten with the need to see her smile like that for the rest of his life—which he knew was irrational and could not happen.

It was as if pulling her down on his lap earlier had broken a wall he'd kept erected all week. Now that it had crumbled, he was struggling to keep his feelings for her under control and had been ever since they'd left the cabin for this last activity.

Since the ranch didn't host rodeos during the winter months, Emberly had wanted to recreate one for him as much as she was able. First, they'd gone into town and shopped for authentic cowboy gear at an upscale place that had closed just for him. He'd had fun picking out and trying on different items before finally settling on what he was wearing.

They'd returned to the rodeo arena, where some of the staff had set up for the performance. Kade had started with his bull riding, for which he had made a name for himself. Another ranch hand had demonstrated steer wrestling. Then Emberly's cousin Carissa had done barrel racing.

Apparently Carissa was extremely talented in training horses. She came from a branch of the McQuaids that had been interested in taming the mustangs that had once roamed the high country freely.

Emberly had explained that Carissa's side of the family owned an enormous ranch on the Front Range near Colorado Springs. But she'd moved up to Healing Springs shortly after she'd discovered she was pregnant. Without the father of the baby involved, she had stayed after the baby was born and gave horse-riding lessons at a ranch near town.

"And that's how we do it here," Emberly called as she directed Princess Max's way, avoiding the few muddy spots left from the snow earlier in the week.

Good heavens. She was stunning. He may as well admit his thought. Whether holding a lasso or dressed in lace, she was always stunning. But for some reason today, now, she was especially enticing.

"What did you think?" she called.

"You were fabulous." He almost added the word *darling* but caught himself just in time.

She reined in only a foot away, her vibrance and youth and beauty so intense that he wanted to reach for her and pull her onto his lap again.

She eyed his lap, as if thinking the same thing.

His pulse spurted. Surely not.

She cleared her throat. "In this sort of situation, you could lavish a little more praise, but only if it's genuine."

"Of course." He thought back to a moment ago, when she'd held the rope in perfect tension above her head. "I could watch you ride a horse and rope steer all night." Did he sound too passionate?

Her eyes narrowed on him. "No flattery. You know that's one of the rules."

He sat up straighter. "I am not flattering you. I meant exactly what I said. I thoroughly enjoyed your performance and would love watching you do it again."

"Really?" Did her voice hold a note of hope?

"Yes. Really." He was not sure why his own voice dropped lower. "The truth is, I love watching you do everything."

This time her eyes widened.

"Did I say too much this time?"

"Did you mean it?"

"Absolutely." Once again, the lines were starting to blur between the pretense and the truth of how he was feeling for her. Even though he'd told himself he would put an end to the flirtatious lessons she was giving him, he hadn't been able to make himself do so yet, and he wasn't sure why.

She cocked her head toward the arena. "So, do you want to try any of the stunts?"

"If I do, I shall only make a complete fool of myself."

"I promise I won't laugh."

Before he could say anything, a voice behind him answered, "No, Emberly. We don't let the guests try the stunts, and you know it."

Max shifted to find Tyler standing behind him, his thick arms crossed. The oldest McQuaid was in his usual cowboy hat, flannel, jeans, and cowboy boots. He was decisive, commanding, and a clear leader, not unlike Max. But he was also much more intense, somewhat gruff, and certainly not warm and welcoming.

"I think you're done here," Tyler said in a clipped tone, as though he didn't approve of Emberly's private rodeo in the first place.

Emberly visibly bristled. "We were fine, Ty. We were just doing some practicing like we've done plenty of times."

A muscle in Tyler's jaw ticked. "Fine. But it's time to

put an end to this."

"Why?"

"You've given your guest preferential treatment all week, but this is taking things too far."

Max's gut tightened at Tyler's tongue-lashing. Emberly did not deserve his censure. "Emberly is not to blame for any of this."

"Max," she started.

"'Tis true. When you texted the activities that we could do today, I chose this."

"I wanted to do it too."

"Regardless, I have encouraged more than necessary." As he spoke, he leveled his gaze at Tyler. "So do not take your irritation out on her."

"Don't worry." Tyler held his ground. "I'm irritated at you too."

"Very well." Max climbed down from the fence. His new leather boots were shiny and clean and completely out of place next to Tyler's scuffed and worn boots that had likely seen a great deal of hard work. "I hope the irritation will very soon be replaced by satisfaction when I return home and do my best to promote your ranch in my country and around the world."

Tyler's expression remained hard. "You'll return and never contact Emberly again?"

"Ty!" Emberly began to dismount her horse. "Stop right now."

Max was not sure how to answer Tyler. All week, he had been telling himself his friendship with Emberly was confined to one week, that when he went back to his normal life, he would be busy and would forget about her. He had even tried to convince himself earlier that he could never do a long-distance relationship.

But was it possible they could stay in contact? Perhaps text once in a while?

Tyler pinned his gaze on Max, clearly waiting for a response to his demand.

Max steeled his shoulders. "While I appreciate your concern for your sister, I do not make a practice of letting others dictate how I handle my friendships."

"Friendship?" Tyler snorted. "From what I've seen, this thing goes beyond friendship."

"Ty, that's enough." Emberly's voice held exasperation.

"Truthfully, *this thing* is not your concern." Max had already experienced such interference once in his life with Ava, and he refused to allow it to happen again.

Tyler took a step back, then nodded at the beautiful home on the hill, the one where the McQuaid family lived. "Dad wants to see you."

Emberly shook her head. "Tell him I'll stop by later."

"He wants to see both you and Max." Tyler's voice sounded ominous.

Emberly hesitated.

"I am happy to do so." Max had not yet met the head of the family, and he was not afraid of an encounter. He had no doubt T.W. McQuaid had been kept apprised of his and Emberly's doings over the week. Did T.W. wish to scold him for spending so much time with Emberly? If so, why bother now that his visit was almost over?

"You don't have to, Max." Emberly pinched the bridge of her nose. He'd noticed she did so when she was in a stressful situation. Was she resistant to taking him to see her father? Was that stressful to her?

"If you prefer that I not meet your father, then I shall accept your decision."

"No, that's not it at all," she replied quickly. "I just don't want you to feel the pressure."

"Have no worry on my account. I am not afraid to meet your father."

She studied his face and then nodded. "Okay, if you're sure."

"I am certain."

Max drew in a steadying breath. He was in charge of his relationships, and if—and that was only *if*—he wanted to pursue something with Emberly, he would not let Tyler or her father interfere. He would not even let his own father stop him.

Of course, Max had never concerned himself with choosing a wife who would please his father. But after his father's role in shunning Ava, Max was even less inclined.

In fact, for a while during those days when he had been reeling with the pain of losing Ava, he had contemplated selecting someone his father did not approve of simply to serve his comeuppance.

Max no longer had the burning need for revenge. But what would his father say if he became engaged to Emberly? Not only was she a commoner, but she was a simple American without any fame or fortune. While that didn't bother Max in the least, what would his father think about a gun-shooting, lasso-throwing cowgirl becoming queen of their nation?

Max almost smiled at how an engagement to Emberly would surprise his father. Perhaps his father would regret not letting him marry Ava, who, although not royalty, at least lived in his country, spoke the language, and was familiar with royal ways.

Yes, a woman such as Emberly would likely be a thorn in his father's flesh. And no doubt he would discourage the union, perhaps try to prevent it.

No, if Max were ever to seriously contemplate such a wild plan, he would have to take drastic measures to ensure the union occurred. Most likely he would need to elope.

Elope?

Max almost scoffed aloud. What was wrong with him? His thoughts were entirely out of line. He was quite possibly losing his mind. Just because his feelings toward

Emberly were heightened, it did not warrant his fantasizing about marrying her. He'd probably only done so because he was growing more desperate with the looming deadline of his birthday.

He would not actually consider a permanent union with Emberly. More importantly, she would never consider a union with him. If he even hinted at it, she would laugh in his face.

Truly, he was mad for even thinking about it, and he would be better off putting such far-fetched notions from his mind.

10

Emberly was more than a little irritated again at her family's interference. But as she stepped into the great room with Max, she tamped down the frustration.

"There's my girl!" Dad called from his recliner near the wall of windows and sliding glass doors. The lamp on the barrel-style end table cast a soft glow over him, taking away some of the pallor and haggardness that had been plaguing him for months.

"Hi, Dad." She made her way toward him. "Where's Mom?" The spacious kitchen to the side of the great room was tidy but empty, the dinner pans already washed and drying in a rack on the counter.

Dad had his feet up with his laptop open in front of him. His dark hair had more silver than it ever had before, but he was still a handsome McQuaid man. "Anson has the night off, so your mom took Wyatt to Cub Scouts."

That accounted for why the old cowboy-turned-housekeeper was nowhere in sight, and why Tyler's miniature-lookalike son was also not racing around the house like he usually was.

Emberly leaned down and gave her dad a hug, trying to ignore how bony his shoulders felt. Several Excel spreadsheets were open on his screen, which meant he was going over the ranch's budget. Was he trying to figure out if they had enough yet to purchase the new land and expand the ranch's operations?

"Don't worry," came Kinsey's voice from down the hallway near Dad's bedroom. "T.W.'s not alone. I'm here."

Dad expelled a sigh. "I told her she didn't have to come over, but she insisted."

Tyler's fiancée, Kinsey, was a nurse and had moved into her own apartment last fall. It was in Healing Springs so that she could oversee the new clinic she'd recently opened, giving their small town its own medical center. Their wedding was planned for July, and Tyler hoped to have their house finished by then. He was building it on a parcel of land only a mile or so away from the family home. Of course, Dad had offered to move out so that Tyler, Kinsey, and Wyatt could have the big home for themselves. But Tyler had wanted to give Kinsey a home of their own.

"I promise I won't bother you guys," Kinsey called.

"We don't mind." Emberly liked her future sister-in-law. She was not only the perfect match for Tyler, but she fit well into their family with her direct and no-nonsense personality.

Dad was peering over the rim of his reading glasses at Max, who'd stepped up beside Emberly. "And you must be Max."

"I am." Max held out a hand, looking as suave and gentlemanly as usual, even though he was decked out in Western gear. "I am pleased to meet you, sir."

"Same here." Dad accepted Max's hand and exchanged a hearty handshake. "I've been hearing a lot about you this week."

"I do hope it was not all bad."

"Course not." Dad leaned back and closed his laptop. "Besides, I know better than to believe everything my sons tell me when it comes to the men Emberly dates."

"I'm not dating Max."

"Darlin', if what you've been doing this week isn't dating, I don't know what is."

Emberly rolled her eyes. "Da-ad."

"According to both Tyler and Kade, you've spent hours every day with your new man—"

"He's also not my *new man*." Dad's insinuations were mortifying. She should have listened to her internal warning that he would end up embarrassing her one way or another. "I've been Max's concierge this week. That's all."

"That's all?" Dad smiled up at her, his eyes twinkling. "I think I know what falling in love looks and sounds like."

"Oh my." Emberly buried her face in her hands, wishing the floor would swallow her up. If she protested, her dad would say something about how her objections only supported his claim. "You're impossible. You know that, don't you?"

Her dad chuckled.

She dropped her hands, but she didn't dare look at Max and gauge his reaction to the conversation.

"Your daughter has been wonderful, Mr. McQuaid—"

"Call me T.W."

"T.W.," Max said smoothly. "Emberly is truly a special woman, and I am afraid I did monopolize her time."

Wonderful? Special? Emberly wanted to savor his words, but now was not the time. Not with Dad watching her and assuming she was in love with Max.

"From what I've heard, Emberly enjoyed her time with you."

Emberly shook her head. "I showed Max my favorite activities, so of course I enjoyed the time with him."

Max arched a brow at her as though asking her to be honest if he'd been too demanding of her.

Of course he hadn't been. She was strong enough to stand up for herself and wouldn't have done anything she didn't want to. Hopefully he knew that by now. She bumped her shoulder against his arm. "He's tried to keep up with me, but he has a lot yet to learn."

"That's why I called you both here." Dad's gaze bounced back and forth between them. "I wanted to see if Max would like to stay longer, maybe for another week."

"What?" Emberly's mouth nearly dropped open. What was her dad doing? If she didn't know better, she'd almost think he was trying to set her up with Max. But why would he do that when he didn't know anything about Max other than what her nosy brothers had said?

"I don't know what your schedule is like, Max," Dad continued, "but maybe you can work remotely or rearrange your schedule to free up your workload."

After the past week of taking so much time away from work, Max was probably feeling the pressure to get back to business. But instead of a polite refusal, he slid his hands into his pockets and didn't immediately respond.

Her heart thudded an extra beat. Did she want him to stay? If she was completely honest, thoughts of him driving away from the ranch had flooded her mind with a strange sadness that he would walk out of her life forever.

She'd known all along that the time with him was temporary and would soon be over. Maybe because of that, she'd allowed herself to let go of reservations and just have fun with him. She'd had nothing to lose in being herself and making the most of the time.

Or maybe she had more to lose than she'd realized . . . like maybe her heart.

Max met her gaze, his silvery-green eyes turning serious. "What do you think?"

Was he really considering her dad's idea? That was ludicrous, wasn't it? Why would he want to stay here when he had a busy life waiting for him? And there was Sarah. Wasn't he planning to go home and attempt to repair his relationship with the duchess?

"Would you be open to the idea?" Max's gaze seemed to probe deeper.

"You've told me how much work you've put off this week—"

"I can delegate it. I have already had to do that with some of the newest portfolios, and I shall do it again."

Was he admitting he wanted to take up her dad's offer? If so, was it because he wanted to spend more time with her?

The prospect of getting to be with him a little longer was really appealing. She'd grown to admire and respect him as a person and as a prince. Not only was he personable, kind, and enjoyable to be with, but he was intelligent, compassionate, and determined and would make a great king of his nation one day.

But what would his staying at the ranch longer accomplish? It wasn't as if anything could happen between them. Not when he was a prince and far out of her league. Even if he hadn't been a prince and had simply been a wealthy man, they were two different people from two different walks of life and two different parts of the world.

"I can tell you want to stay." Dad was studying Max's face. "So why not just say yes?"

"Your offer is very kind, to be sure." Max's mannerisms set him apart from the ordinary man. Could her dad see that, and was he wondering more about Max's story? "But I do not wish to annoy Emberly if she prefers to have me leave."

"Of course I don't."

"So you would like me to stay?"

Did she dare say so? A part of the truth was that she didn't want him to leave at all, ever. A part of her wanted to go on spending her afternoons and evenings with him indefinitely.

There had been a few times where an attraction had seemed to flare to life between them. The key word was *seemed*. She'd caught him looking at her a time or two with something more in his eyes than friendship—or so she thought. And she'd felt a magnetic tug toward him once in a while, especially when he'd pulled her down on his lap. He'd only been practicing, but it had felt charged, making her want to linger there against him.

As tempting as it had been to let herself get carried

away with a man as handsome as Max, she'd kept good boundaries.

Max was still waiting for her response, his expression growing more serious. "If you would like me to go tomorrow, just say so."

"That's not it." With her dad staring up at her expectantly, she suddenly felt on display. "Maybe we can have a private word out on the deck." Away from her dad's pressure.

"Now, darlin'," Dad started, "you don't need to overthink this. I was just hoping Max would stay so I could get to know him better."

She leveled a look at her dad. Why did he want to get to know Max better?

Dad only smiled. "Tyler already told me the Antelope is booked up, as are all the other cabins. So Max and his staff can stay here in the house."

"That may not be private enough—"

"Thank you for the kind offer." Max smiled back at her dad. "I would enjoy the chance to get to know you better too."

"Then it's settled." Dad relaxed against his chair, looking way too smug.

Emberly huffed, then started toward the sliding glass door that led to the deck. Max followed her without any prompting. As they stepped out, the darkness of the early evening enveloped them, along with the chill of the mountain temperatures. Thankfully, she was still wearing her coat, and so was Max.

She closed the door and then crossed to the railing. She leaned against it and stared at the western range, where a golden line from the sun's last rays outlined the rugged peaks.

After a moment, she felt Max beside her.

"You do not seem sure if you would like me to extend my visit."

She blew out a tight breath. "What would be the point, Max?" She may as well be as blunt as always. "We can spend more time together, but it won't change the outcome of your visit."

"What outcome is that?"

"We'll be parting ways tomorrow or in a few days. Either way, we'll say our goodbyes and likely never see each other again. So why drag things out?"

"We have become friends, have we not?"

"I think so, yes."

"Then perhaps we can remain friends, stay in contact, send each other advice, good or bad . . ." His voice hinted at humor.

She couldn't hold back a smile. What was it about him that made her smile so easily? "My advice is always good. Remember that."

"You have not led me astray yet."

"And I won't."

He was silent a beat. "This time together, you, your ranch, it has given me the space away from my life that I have needed."

"I'm so glad." She really was happy he'd benefited from the ranch experience. She couldn't fathom what his normal life was like as the CEO of the world's wealthiest bank and heir to the throne of his country. The pressure had to be heavy and the duties unending.

"I should like to spend a few more days here . . . with you. If you are agreeable."

"With me?"

"Yes. With you."

"And what if I tell you I'm busy and assigning you a new concierge?"

"Then I shall demand that I have only you."

Was his voice slightly husky, or was she only imagining it? "Demand?"

"I will not ask this time." His voice was low and definitely husky.

Her stomach flipped with an anticipation she didn't want to feel.

"Take the time off too."

"You're bossy, you know that?"

"When I know what I want, why bother with niceties?"

Had he really just said he wanted her? No, he didn't mean it in a romantic way. He meant he wanted her to remain his personal tour guide. And she knew she was going to take the time off—not just because he'd suggested it but because she wanted to be with him. In fact, she wanted to be with him much more than she dared to admit.

11

Max's father was not pleased with his decision to extend his visit to Colorado.

Sitting on a stool at the kitchen counter, Max closed the exchange of texts and placed his phone face down. His father had complained that Max was wasting time. According to Father, he was *gallivanting around* and *avoiding his responsibilities* instead of being home and *planning for his future*.

Father had asked him pointedly: *"If you are not willing to be responsible, then stop delaying and abdicate to Alex."*

Stop delaying and abdicate.

Was that what he should do? Abdicating would certainly take away the pressure to marry.

Yet, all his life, Max had prepared to be the next king. He had practiced for it, lived for it, and dreamed of it. He'd had the education and training to be a king. He even had the heart for it in a way that Alex never would.

The truth was, Max did not wish to abdicate, not only because he was ready and capable of leading his country but also because he was unaccustomed to admitting defeat. He had clung to the hope that he would discover a way to make the situation work in his favor, and he was still clinging to that hope, although less tenaciously.

"All set for the excursion?" T.W. asked as he shuffled from the hallway into the kitchen.

After staying in the family home for the past two nights, Max had spent enough time with T.W. to know he was a smart and savvy man who had accomplished great things with Healing Springs Ranch in his lifetime.

Emberly had been right about his love for his wife. He was love-crazy for Leah—so much so that Leah adored him in return. Max had been watching the way T.W. interacted with Leah, and he'd witnessed the older man putting into practice many of the examples Emberly had shared. T.W.'s genuine, unconditional, and comprehensive love was truly inspiring, and Max had determined more than ever to facilitate that legacy of love in his own marriage—even though he was not a McQuaid.

'Twas clear T.W. also cared deeply for his children. He expected them to love God, love family, and work hard. He was very open about his desire for each of his children to have fulfilling marriages with loving spouses.

With both Tyler and Brock having fallen in love, he believed Emberly was next.

"She needs someone who isn't afraid of her sass and who appreciates her strength," T.W. had told him yesterday when they'd been eating breakfast together. "She also needs a man who isn't intimidated by her brothers."

Strangely enough, Max had wanted to claim that he fulfilled all those requirements, that he liked Emberly's sass and strength. They were among the qualities he liked best about her. He was also utterly unfazed by her brothers, especially Tyler, who seemed the most perturbed by Max's decision to remain on the ranch through midweek.

"I'm sure Emberly already warned you to dress in layers," T.W. said as he approached the refrigerator. "You can always take off the layers if you get too warm, but you can't do anything if you get cold."

"Emberly did indeed relay that advice." With all the layers, Max was starting to overheat as he waited for Emberly to arrive at the house so that they could begin their snowshoeing trip.

Max was not a novice to snowshoeing, and he was looking forward to hiking into the wilderness and getting to see more of the backcountry. More than that, he wanted to enjoy one more day with Emberly.

She had taken the time away from her work and spent

the past two full days with him. They had cross-country skied, hiked to a wildlife viewing area, taken one of the ranch's photography classes, relaxed in the spa and hot spring, and eaten plenty of excellent food.

Today, on Max's final extra day here, T.W. had suggested they hike out to the cabin his father had built in the Tarryall Range near Cowboy Peak. The cabin wasn't accessible by vehicle but could be reached in the summer by ATVs and in the winter by snowmobiles. The place was apparently rustic compared with the cabins on the ranch and didn't have running water or electricity. But T.W. had talked fondly of how he and Leah had gone there often over the years for a romantic night or two alone.

From the base of Cowboy Peak, the hike to the cabin by snowshoe would only take three or four hours. Emberly had made the journey many times and knew the way well. But she'd planned for Winzig to accompany them on a snowmobile in order to carry in supplies for lunch. Although she had not explicitly stated that the snowmobile would also provide an emergency way out of the mountains if anything happened to them, Max suspected that was also part of her motivation.

When Braun had learned of the expedition, he'd insisted on having a snowmobile of his own and joining them. Among his many eccentric interests, Braun was an avid snocross follower. He watched the snowmobile racing competitions and knew the statistics of the top contenders for the upcoming Winter X Games. Although Braun admitted he had actually never managed a snowmobile himself, he was giddy about the prospect of riding one, and Max hadn't the heart to deny him.

T.W. poured himself a glass of orange juice, then paused to peer out the large kitchen windows to the western range. "Looks like we'll get some snow today."

Max shifted on his stool at the center counter and took in the magnificent vista—the low clouds that touched the peaks. The clouds did appear heavy and full of moisture. But the rest of the landscape was bathed in brilliant sunlight with blue skies overhead.

"Emberly has been keeping an eye on the weather forecast for today." Max appreciated her attention to detail in all the activities they had done.

"She's smart." T.W. took a sip of his juice. "Even if you get a little snow later, she'll be able to handle it."

"She is quite smart and independent." Among a hundred other excellent qualities.

T.W. drank more of his juice before setting the glass onto the counter and turning his full attention onto Max. "I've appreciated getting to know you. You're a fine young man, Max."

"Thank you." Max had the sudden feeling that their conversation was taking a serious turn, and he braced himself for T.W.'s assessment.

"I like you a lot," T.W. continued. "And I think you're perfect for Emberly."

Perfect for Emberly? Max's racing mind came to an abrupt halt. What was T.W. saying? "But . . . ?"

T.W. chuckled softly. "There's no *but*."

Was T.W. telling him that he would support a relationship with his daughter? That could not be true, could it?

"I wasn't kidding when I mentioned that you and Emberly are falling in love with each other."

T.W. had said something about that during their introductions, but Max had not taken him seriously, had assumed he was teasing Emberly. Although Max did not want to contradict T.W., he had to correct the man. Max liked Emberly, admired her, was attracted to her—a great deal, actually. But love?

"I do think it is rather soon to conclude that we are falling in love. After all, we have known each other less than two weeks."

"At your age, two weeks is plenty of time to know if you've found the one."

Max could not quite believe he was having this conversation with T.W. It seemed slightly presumptuous and forward, but he had learned the McQuaids were not reticent. They spoke directly about most issues.

Surely, then, T.W. would not mind candidness in return. "I do not believe in *the one* philosophy of finding a spouse. Nor do I believe I must find my *soulmate* or forever relegate myself to unhappiness."

"I don't either."

Max paused. "Is that so?"

"Course we'll feel more attracted to certain people than others." T.W. was still studying Max intently. "But once we decide on a person, then they become *the one*, and it's our lifelong job to turn them into our *soulmate*."

Max liked that reasoning. "Is that what you have done with your wife?"

T.W. smiled softly in the direction of the lower level, where Leah was using their top-of-the-line exercise equipment to work out. "Yep. I've made it my life's mission to make her feel cherished every single day."

"That is quite the noble undertaking."

"It's nothing less than what God designed—that a husband love his wife so completely that he would die for her."

Everything T.W. was saying made complete sense. He could understand now why Emberly respected her father and his advice so much. "So you believe I can love Emberly the way you love Leah?" Once the question was out, Max felt foolish for uttering it. He had speculated privately about a future with Emberly, but it was not something he was ready to give voice to, especially to T.W.

"Forgive me," he said quickly before T.W. could reply. "I am overreaching—"

"Nope. You're fine. I'd like to hash this out before she gets here."

Hash this out? Max wasn't familiar with the phrase.

"It's real obvious you both care for each other," T.W. continued. "Fact is, I've never seen Emberly as taken with a man as she is with you."

"Not even Ryan?"

T.W. scoffed. "Ryan didn't have enough backbone to hold up against Emberly's brothers. But yours is made of steel."

Max's pulse was suddenly pounding faster. Was T.W. correct about Emberly being more taken with him than with any other man? She had not said anything about liking him, nor had she crossed the line of friendship that had been established.

"I can tell you're just as taken with her."

Max wanted to deny T.W. After all, this was not the sort of conversation he was accustomed to having—talking with a father so openly. But if T.W. could be direct and vulnerable, Max could make the same effort, could he not?

"I shall admit," he said slowly, "I am attracted to her, and I do admire her greatly. She is an incredible person."

T.W.'s smile widened. "Then maybe you should decide she is your one and only."

"I should not like to rush into something and make a mistake."

"I know plenty of couples who waited months, even years, dating each other so they wouldn't rush and make a mistake. But after they were married, they claimed they made a mistake anyway."

"I understand that the length of knowing a person cannot be a deciding factor in a relationship. But taking one's time cannot hurt, can it?"

T.W. shrugged nonchalantly. "Sometimes people delay because they say they need to get to know each other better. But the truth is, a lot of those people don't really dig deeper into each other's lives, even with more time. So in my opinion, *quantity* of time isn't as important as *quality*."

Deep down, Max knew T.W. had a good point. After all, Max had gotten to know Emberly more thoroughly in a week and a half than he had known Sarah in the many months they had dated.

At the clatter of a truck rumbling up the driveway behind the house, Max looked out the window to see Emberly arriving with a trailer carrying the two snowmobiles. T.W.'s expression again turned earnest. "Guess what I'm trying to say, Max, is that I give you my blessing if you decide you want to make Emberly *your one*."

A strange relief whispered through Max, although he was not sure why, since he had no plan—at least yet—to make Emberly *his one*. As soon as the relief came, so did a prick of guilt. Would T.W. be so gracious if he knew Max's real identity as a prince? He had the feeling T.W. probably would not let such news impress or influence him. Yet how could Max accept T.W.'s blessing to have a relationship with Emberly if he had not yet been completely honest?

T.W. cast a glance toward the back hallway, likely knowing this personal time together was rapidly coming to an end. "I'm mighty biased, but I also know Emberly will be a real treasure to the man who claims her."

Max could not argue with that statement—not in the least. Emberly was one of the most incredible women he had ever met. Even if he decided to *claim* her at some point, that did not guarantee she would want him.

The back door rattled.

"She has not made mention of her feelings toward me," Max whispered hastily.

"Guess you have some work to do today to make sure her feelings for you are real clear."

"Hello?" came her call in the hallway.

"In here, darlin'," T.W. called.

Max's mind was spinning with everything he and T.W. had just talked about, likely one of the most honest conversations he had ever had with anyone—except the part where he left out he was a prince.

Even so, the exchange had given him a great deal to ponder during this last day with Emberly. It certainly made him want to test if she might be interested in more than just friendship and consider a future with him.

A future with him.

The very thought was overwhelming, but as she stepped into the room in her heavy gear and with flushed cheeks, her beauty and vibrance and energy made him breathless. He had to hold himself back from going right over to her and proposing on the spot.

He was certifiably crazy. But he did not care one ounce. He was indeed falling in love with Emberly McQuaid, and he could no longer deny it.

12

"I told Emberly I didn't want her going on this hike." Tyler stalked into the kitchen. "And she's refusing to listen."

"I've done this hike at least two dozen times in my life." Emberly had already explained herself to Tyler when she'd been hooking up the snowmobile trailer. But he was refusing to listen. "The heaviest snow is coming later in the day, and we'll be back before it hits."

Tyler paused in the doorway and shot Max a narrowed look before shifting his attention to their dad.

She'd texted Max to be ready early today so they could get a good start, and he'd replied that he was eager to go. He'd obviously been talking with T.W. when she'd entered the kitchen, and from the sheepish look on both their faces, she could guess she'd been the topic of their conversation.

That was fine. She'd ask Max later what embarrassing

information her dad had said this time. Because he'd been telling Max all kinds of things about her childhood and her past since the day Max and Braun and Winzig had moved out of their cabin and into the upstairs rooms.

Max's silvery-green eyes lingered over her with something that sent extra warmth into her blood. Was he looking at her possessively? Or with desire? Or both?

"Tell her not to go," Tyler pleaded with Dad.

Dad shrugged. "I was the one who suggested the hike."

"Why on earth would you do that?"

Emberly couldn't keep from smirking at her brother. Yes, actually, Dad had mentioned the hike yesterday. They'd gotten more snow a day or so ago, and enough remained in the lower elevations to make snowshoeing fun instead of a chore.

"Why are you encouraging this?" Tyler waved a hand between her and Max. "Especially a trip like this where they'll be alone for hours."

She huffed. "We won't be alone. Braun and Winzig are coming."

"See, alone. Those two are *his* right-hand men." Tyler cocked his head at Max.

"In the face of danger," Max cut in, "I would rather have my right-hand men defend Emberly than myself."

Tyler didn't acknowledge Max and instead leveled his glare at Emberly. "You're not going."

Her frustration with her brothers, especially Tyler, was growing unbearable, so much so that she'd slept restlessly last night. She understood that they still viewed her as their little sister and someone they needed to protect. But their attitude toward Max was unacceptable, especially since he'd done nothing for which they could fault him. He'd been above reproach in every way.

She glared back at Tyler. "Stop bossing me around."

"Maybe I wouldn't need to if you were thinking rationally about things."

"I am thinking rationally."

Tyler released an exasperated sigh before turning to face Max. "If you want to prove yourself to us, then cancel the hike and do something here at the ranch, where Emberly can be supervised better."

"I don't need your constant supervision," she cut in. Ryan had complained a lot about her brothers, especially how they didn't seem to like him or trust him. She knew they'd been overbearing, but had they been this bad? And was that why Ryan had grown tired of being with her?

Maybe she should have stood up to her brothers more often. Maybe she shouldn't have defended them as much as she had. Maybe she should have broken free of their meddling ways much sooner. If she had, maybe she and Ryan would've had more of a chance.

Whatever the case, she couldn't let Tyler drive Max away, and a mounting desperation inside told her that if she didn't do something, that was exactly what would happen again.

"What do you say, Max?" Tyler persisted.

Max had been quietly taking in the whole argument. What did he think? That he wanted to escape from the sibling problems? That her family was too much of a hassle?

As his eyes met hers, he seemed to be conveying that everything was all right. "Listen, Tyler," he started. He had a haughtiness about him, even a dangerous glint in his eyes. "I do not need to prove myself to you or anyone. Emberly and I are adults, and we will make our own choices. If she decides to stay at the ranch today, I shall enjoy her company here. But if she would still like to take the hike, then I shall relish every moment of that as well."

Emberly's heart melted at his every word. She loved that he was taking her side and letting her choose what she wanted to do. And the choice was easy. This time, she wouldn't let her brothers scare away someone she cared about.

"Everything is ready." She cocked her head to the back door and the truck waiting on the driveway.

"Fabulous." Max started toward her. "I am ready too."

As they approached the door, Tyler didn't move.

For a long second, Max locked eyes with him.

Would the two actually have a fistfight?

Tyler finally took a step back so they could pass by. She didn't waste any more time. She grabbed Max's hand and practically dragged him from the house.

Braun and Winzig were already waiting in the cab of the truck when she and Max stepped outside. The food for their picnic lunch was packed, as well as a few supplies that the cabin might need.

During the drive to Cowboy Peak, Emberly kept their conversations light to ease the tension that had built during the interaction with Tyler. She wanted to make the most of every moment they had left. Thankfully, Max seemed to have the same attitude.

As they reached the trailhead, Braun and Winzig loaded up the snowmobiles with their lunch and supplies and led the way slowly while she and Max plodded along behind. With the sun shining, the snow in the lower elevations had turned slushy and made the hiking more strenuous. It wasn't until they started up a gradual incline in a ravine that the snow became more powdery and easier to cross.

All the while they hiked, they talked like they usually did. This time she needed to vent about her brothers. Although she loved her family and knew they loved her, she was becoming more convinced that she needed to find a way to show them she was an adult and could make her own decisions.

She and Max rested at several spots along the way, the

last one being a lake that was frozen over but still picturesque with the snow covering it. The sun had disappeared behind the clouds, but the misty sky made the mountainside even prettier.

The cabin was only a short hike after that. When she and Max broke into the clearing, she paused to admire the cozy one-story log home with its wide front porch, set against the mountainside. Winzig and Braun had already arrived and shoveled a path to the door, uncovered the wood pile under the overhang, and started a fire in the stove. Braun was busy sweeping out the cabin, and Winzig was hauling in a large pot of snow to melt for water for their coffee.

She had fun showing the cabin to Max and explaining that it had been constructed to resemble the one the original Wyatt McQuaid had built on his homestead in the 1860s. It had an open front room with one half containing a couch and love seat, big soft rugs, and a small bookshelf filled with old books and a few games. The other side of the room held a trestle-style table with benches. A simple hutch stood near the stove and was filled with utensils and staple food items. Pots and pans hung above the old-fashioned wood-burning stove, which held a pour-over coffee maker.

Another room at the back of the cabin had a double bed and a bunk bed. Though her parents carried in their bedding whenever they hiked up to the cabin, a trunk against one wall held an assortment of blankets, sheets, and pillows.

The windows were dusty but solid and had been updated over recent years. The shingle roof had also been replaced to make the cabin a place guests could stay in in any weather, although without electricity, running water, internet, or reliable cell phone service, most people kept their visits short.

A light snow had begun to fall by the time they sat down to enjoy the delicious meal Chef Vivalda had prepared for them. Afterward, with their socks, shoes, and mittens still drying from the wet trek through slush, she and Max sat together on the couch and talked more about what life must have been like so long ago without all the modern conveniences they took for granted.

The interior had grown warm, and when Max stepped away for a few minutes to speak with Braun at the table, her restless night caught up with her, and she dozed off.

The banging of the door woke her, and she bolted upright to find that someone had covered her with a blanket and positioned her head on a couch pillow. She wasn't sure how much time had passed, but she never napped long, never had the time for it.

She brushed a strand from her face that had come loose from her braid. At the rattle of one of the windowpanes, her attention shifted to find snow plastered to the glass. From the little she could see of the outside, the snow was falling rapidly.

Urgency prodded her. With the snow coming down so hard, they needed to get out of the mountains and to a lower elevation where the conditions might not be as severe.

"We need to go." She pushed up from the couch to find that she was alone inside. The fire in the stove was still blazing. Someone had brought in more firewood and added to the stack that was already there, because the newer pieces were damp and covered with snow.

She crossed to the door in her bare feet, only to find that the puncheon wood floor was wet—likely from the tromping in and out. Regardless, she pushed at the door. It hardly budged. It was almost as if the wind had an invisible hand holding it closed and trapping her inside.

They had to go before they were trapped in the mountains.

She finally wrestled the door open, and as she stepped outside, a gust slapped her and snow swirled against her face so that she could hardly see a foot from the porch. She squinted in the direction of the path that led to the nearby lake.

Nothing was visible through the blowing snow.

She crossed the wide front porch and caught sight of Max with Winzig and Braun, bundled up by the snowmobiles. The snow sank up to her ankles from the drift already forming on the porch. From what she could tell, between three or four inches of fresh snow had fallen in the time she'd been resting.

Exactly how long had she been asleep? She glanced down at her watch to find that it was only 1:30 p.m. With the hike down not taking quite as long as the hike up, they still had plenty of time to return to the trailhead before darkness settled. They would be back to the ranch in time for dinner, where she planned to prove to Tyler that he'd been wrong about mistrusting her to go on the hike with Max.

But a sinking feeling inside told her that, regardless of the early afternoon hour, time wouldn't be their enemy today. No, the weather would be.

The storm had arrived sooner than the weather app had predicted, and it was a doozy of a storm, with gusty winds, heavy snowfall, and whiteout conditions.

Did they dare try to leave now and make it down before more snow accumulated? Or were the conditions already too dangerous?

With the soles of her feet stinging from the cold and her body starting to shake, she knew she needed to go back inside and get on her gear before venturing out. The issue was that she didn't want anyone leaving without her. They weren't experienced in the mountains like she was.

"Max!" she called.

The wind whipped her voice away.

"Max!" she shouted louder.

Somehow he seemed to hear her—or perhaps he sensed her presence—because he glanced her way. At the sight of her on the porch, he said something curt to Winzig and Braun, and then he started toward her, struggling against the wind and the snow to keep from slipping and falling.

As he started up the steps and took in her condition, a scowl creased his forehead. He hurried his pace as much as he was able. When he reached her, he scooped her up into his arms. Snow covered his coat and ski pants, and it crusted his eyebrows and the strands of his hair hanging out from his winter hat. Cold radiated from him, but he was solid and his presence reassuring.

"What are you doing?" she asked as he secured her against his chest.

"You should not be out here like this." He began tromping toward the door.

"I don't need you to carry me."

"I know." He kicked the door open with his boot and crossed to the couch she'd just abandoned. Winzig and Braun were close on his heels and shut the cabin door against the flurry of snow and cold.

Max lowered her to the cushions. "We were thinking that maybe we could double up on the snowmobiles and try to make it down. What do you think?"

She appreciated that he was asking for her advice and wasn't assuming he knew better than she did.

"Unfortunately, with the whiteout conditions, I don't think it's safe for any of us to go right now." Her teeth were chattering as she spoke, and she wrapped her arms around herself to ward off a shudder.

He grabbed the blanket and draped it around her. "What about the parts of the trail that pass through the woodland? We would have less wind and snow there, would we not?"

"It'd still be difficult to navigate. And with the wind blowing so hard, we'd have to go slow and worry about falling limbs and the chance of hitting them."

He nodded gravely, his face ruddy from the cold and the snowflakes and ice. "Then what do you suggest we do?"

As far as she could tell, they had only one choice. "We wait out the worst of the storm and leave when the wind and snow die down."

"From your experience, how long do you expect the storm will last?"

Both Winzig and Braun were watching her expectantly, as if she had the power to wave a magic wand and make the storm disappear.

She hated to disappoint them, but there wasn't anything she could do. "It will probably last a few more hours at least."

Braun began to unwind a bright red-and-white knitted scarf—one of his own creations. "So we relax for a few hours and leave later in the afternoon?"

"My guess is that by the time it blows over, it'll be too late in the day to start out. I don't want to try the trek down the mountain in the dark."

"But the snowmobiles have headlights."

"Even so, the trail will be snow-covered, and I'd hate for us to make a wrong turn." One wrong turn could be deadly. They could go over a cliff, fall into a ravine, hit a boulder, lose their way, and any number of other things.

The crease in Max's brow hadn't gone away. "Then you suggest we stay overnight?"

"We'll be just fine here for the night. The place is warm, and we have food and water." When she'd opened the cupboard earlier, she'd found canned food, canned coffee grounds, some packages of dried meals, and plenty of matches and lighters. They could melt snow for water and had plenty of wood for fuel. What more did they need?

Braun draped his scarf on a hook near the door, then began to shed his coat. "If we stay, we'll miss our flight tomorrow."

Max straightened and peered out the window that was now frosting over on the inside. "Our flight is the least of my concerns."

"Your father will not be happy," Braun said.

"He is already unhappy."

Emberly wanted to ask Max why his father was

unhappy. Because he'd stayed at the ranch longer than originally planned? "If we leave at sunrise tomorrow, we should be back well before noon. There may still be time to catch your flight in Denver."

"We shall not worry about it." Max's tone held a finality that told her he intended to make the most of the delay. He tucked the blanket around her more securely and then gently touched her chin. "I am able to spend extra time with you. I cannot complain about that in the least."

His caress sent a shaft of warmth through her. "All the more chance to beat you and Winzig in Rummy."

Winzig had been a good sport about playing cards with them over the past week, and now he offered her a smile as he took off his coat.

"Victory will not be yours quite so readily this time." Max's shoulders seemed to relax, and the furrow faded from his brow. "I have improved and have become a staunch competitor."

"We'll see about that." A part of her was actually glad they were snowed in together. She'd been given a little more time with him, and she intended to enjoy every moment.

13

"I insist on sleeping on the couch." Emberly flopped down onto the couch, put up her feet, and crossed her arms.

The oil lantern hanging from the rafter cast a warm glow over the room and over the men, who were still sitting at the table and now staring at her. Winzig had joined her and Max in their games, and Braun had spent the evening creating origami creatures from paper he'd found in the kitchen hutch, apparently another one of his many hobbies.

"It makes sense for the three of you to share a room," she insisted. "And the couch is perfectly comfortable."

"'Tis not as comfortable as the bed." Max stood and began gathering the playing cards.

"It's one night. And I'll be fine."

He shook his head, his frustration palpable.

Braun finished folding the last wing on what appeared

to be a swan. "At least she will stay warmer if she sleeps near the stove."

The stove had pumped out heat all afternoon and evening. At times, it had even grown too toasty. They still had plenty of wood inside to see them through the night, but Braun was right that the back bedroom would be chillier, even with using the blankets in the chest.

"Very well." Max finished stacking the deck. "Perhaps it is the best solution to allow Emberly to be near the source of heat."

The stovepipe rattled, and a whistle of wind made its way under the front door in spite of a rolled-up rug to keep out the draft.

Emberly was praying they would only have to stay one night, but with the way the storm was still raging, she was beginning to worry they might be stuck longer.

The last time she'd gone out with Max to check on the snowfall, they'd barely made it to the edge of the porch with the force of the blowing snow. The steps had been covered in drifts, so they hadn't ventured down. But from what they could tell, at least eight to twelve inches of fresh powder had fallen since the afternoon.

It was still coming down hard and hadn't shown any signs of letting up. As high up on the mountain as they were, they could easily get another foot or two before the storm moved on. That amount would make traveling out of the high elevation difficult, even by snowmobile.

She didn't want to worry about it and borrow trouble. But she also knew that their situation was precarious. No doubt her family was also worried about them since they hadn't returned as scheduled. Without cell phone service, they couldn't call anyone to inform them of the delay. She hoped everyone would realize they'd decided to stay the night rather than hike back down in the storm.

Braun yawned loudly. "Shall we turn in?"

"You and Winzig go ahead." Max began to cross to the stove. "I shall make sure the stove is fed."

"I can do that," Winzig said in German.

"No, I want to," Max replied in German.

"Of course you do." Braun's voice—also in German—was quiet with a note of teasing. "You will do anything to spend more time with her."

"Yes," Max whispered his reply. "But I promise I shall be on my very best behavior."

"Very best?" Braun tsked. "You can kiss her, you know."

"I shall not take advantage of her or the situation."

"Perhaps 'tis less about taking advantage and more about letting her know you have feelings for her."

He had feelings for her? After spending so much time together, she and Max had grown close. But what did Braun mean?

She held her breath and waited for more of their whispered conversation in German.

Braun stifled another yawn. "Just tell her you care about her, Your Highness. And kiss her."

Care about her? Kiss her?

"Go to sleep and say no more." Even though Max's tone was quietly commanding, it also contained a note of affection for Braun.

Emberly ducked her head. They still didn't know she could understand everything they were saying. Should she confess that she could speak German? But then would she have to admit she knew he was a prince? Maybe it was time to come clean about it.

Max finished adding wood to the stove and then made his way to the love seat adjacent to her. As he sat, he stretched his jean-clad legs out in front of him and rested his arms along the edge of the couch behind him.

"Max," she said hesitantly. "I need to tell you something."

"I need to tell you something too." He was taking her in, his eyes wide and the green brightening.

"You go first."

He glanced beyond her to the table, then frowned.

Emberly followed his gaze to find Braun making a kissing motion in the air. Braun quickly pretended he was blowing and swatting at a bug. "This place needs an exterminator."

Emberly tried to hide her smile, but when Max rolled his eyes at Braun, she couldn't keep from chuckling.

After a moment, Max leaned back and released a slow smile.

It took several minutes before Braun and Winzig disappeared into the other room. The dividing wall was thin, and she and Max could hear every sound the two men made as they climbed into their beds and situated themselves. That meant Braun and Winzig would be able to hear everything she and Max said too. But hopefully they would soon be asleep.

"So, what were you going to say?" she whispered.

He looked so relaxed in his jeans and the long-sleeved thermal shirt that had been under the thick wool sweater he'd been wearing earlier. His fair hair was tousled and his face scruffier than usual, so that he was rugged and gentlemanly at the same time, making him look like he half belonged in the Old West and half belonged in a palace.

The cabin was quiet now except for the wind rattling the windows and trees and anything else it could reach.

Max leaned forward suddenly, braced his elbows on his knees, and hung his head.

"I can go first," she offered.

"No." His tone was soft but firm. "I must confess that I have not been completely honest with you about who I am."

She wanted to jump in and tell him that she already knew who he was.

Before she could formulate a response, he lifted his head and looked her in the eyes. "I am the crown prince of Karltenberg."

"Okay."

His eyes widened. "Just okay?"

"Remember that I said I needed to tell you something?"

He pressed his lips together, clearly wanting more of a reaction from her than her *okay*.

"I realized you were a prince from the first day I met you."

"What?" He straightened. "How? Did someone else say something? One of the other bankers?"

"No." She shifted into speaking German so that there would be no doubt in his mind that she knew. "I heard Braun call you Your Highness. And it didn't take much investigating after that to find out who you were."

"I see."

She sat up. "You're irritated at me." She switched back to English now that she'd made her point.

"Yes, you should have told me you knew."

"I could say the same thing of you."

"This is different. You can speak German and overheard our conversations."

"I admit, I felt like I was eavesdropping."

"You were." He stood abruptly. "You deceived me."

She pushed up so that she was standing too. "And you deceived me."

"How could I deceive you when you already knew my true identity?"

"It was still deception since your intention was to hide it from me."

They weren't exactly shouting, but neither were they being quiet anymore. She supposed it was good that Braun and Winzig could hear the truth too.

He stood rigid, his chin high and his shoulders straight. He looked haughty and powerful, like a king. Did royalty practice that kind of stance? Because he had it down to perfection.

He held her gaze for a moment, then blew out a taut breath. "You are right. It was still deception. And I apologize for not telling you sooner."

"And I'm sorry for not telling you sooner too."

"I have no excuse, but I had just hoped to have a private vacation without any paparazzi discovering my whereabouts and disturbing me."

"I heard you say so to Braun, which was one of the reasons why I decided to keep quiet about it."

"What were the other reasons?"

"I admit, I was afraid you'd leave if you knew that I knew."

"I doubt I would have."

"But you didn't know if you could trust me to keep your secret and not gossip about it with others. The news would have spread fast."

"True."

"I didn't want to risk anything happening to spoil the week for you and the rest of the men in the group, especially because Dad and Tyler were so excited about getting international recognition for our ranch."

He slipped his hands into his pockets, and his shoulders seemed to lose their tension.

She expelled a breath. "I hope you understand."

"I do. You had your reasons for staying silent, the same way I had mine. And I cannot condemn you for it."

"Thank you, Max."

He nodded.

Something was off. She could feel it between them, but she couldn't put her finger on what it was. Was he still upset at her?

"I could have at least told you that I knew," she admitted. "But once I decided to let the matter go, I didn't really think about it much."

He didn't respond.

"Besides, what was I supposed to say? 'Good job on the ski hill, and by the way, I know you're a prince'?"

"I do truly understand, Emberly. You were actually quite honorable with your intentions, and I appreciate it."

But did he?

He shifted to glance out the window. The oil lantern above the table was still burning and revealed the drifts of snow now covering all but a small piece of the glass.

Had she ruined her relationship with Max? Would things be different and awkward between them?

A strange desperation began to seep through her. She didn't want their relationship to change, didn't want to lose the connection she had with him, didn't want to lose *him*.

Without giving herself a chance to second-guess herself, she crossed toward him. As she stopped in front of him, he continued to stare out the window.

Boldly, she lifted a hand and cupped his cheek. "Don't be mad at me, okay?"

14

"I am not mad at you." He was not mad at her in the least. Instead, he was stunned at her revelation that she had known who he was from almost the moment she'd met him.

She'd realized he was a prince, and she had not tried to impress him, had not groveled, had not catered to his every whim, had not given him whatever he wanted, had not allowed him to order her around.

Simply put, she hadn't changed who she was because of his royalty. She had been utterly and completely herself while knowing this whole time who he was.

The very thought almost made him weak. Was he relieved? He certainly was flabbergasted. No one had ever treated him as a normal person and an equal, not if they knew he was a prince. Not until Emberly McQuaid.

Even when the attraction between them had flared to life a few times, she had never once pressured him for more in their relationship so that she could further herself—unlike other women he'd dated. She had kept the boundaries between them high, not even hinting that she would like more because she was enamored by the possibility of a royal life.

Was that because she was opposed to it? Maybe she didn't want to be in a relationship with a prince. Maybe she couldn't see herself becoming a future queen. Maybe she had no desire to walk into a way of life so foreign to her own.

A strange sense of panic began to swell inside him. He could no longer deny what had been simmering inside him all day since his conversation with T.W. that morning. He wanted Emberly. More than he'd ever wanted any other woman, even more than Ava. In fact, what he felt for Emberly could not even begin to compare. It went far beyond that long-ago teenage relationship—so much so that he wasn't sure what he'd felt with Ava could even be considered love.

Love?

Yes, indeed.

He shifted so that he was facing Emberly squarely. Her upturned face was wreathed with worry lines, and her brown eyes welled with frustration.

"Something's wrong," she whispered. "I don't want things to change between us just because our secrets are out in the open."

With her hand still upon his cheek, he lifted his hand to her face and gently grazed her cheek. "*Things* must change."

She leaned into his touch. "No."

What other woman would ever tell him no? Not a single one that he'd ever known. "Oh good heavens, I love you." The words came out a growl.

From the other room, Braun tsked happily.

At the same time, Emberly pulled back, her eyes rounding, her lashes fanning out, her beautiful features utterly confused. "What?"

He had not meant to say the words at that precise moment, but now that his declaration was out, he knew it was utterly true. He had fallen in love with this woman. T.W. had already noticed it and acknowledged it. And he had also given Max his blessing to pursue Emberly.

The truth was that he loved Emberly and wanted her in his life forever.

He lifted his other hand so that he was framing her face. "I have fallen in love with you."

She searched his eyes, as though she could not quite believe him.

"I have never loved a woman the way I love you."

He was moving fast. But T.W. had also been right about the timing of love. Max was old enough to know what he wanted and to know love when it came his way. Emberly might not be at the same place yet, but he could win her with the kind of unconditional love she had been talking about and that T.W. exemplified.

"You do not need to reciprocate right now," he whispered. "But I will win you—"

She lifted on her toes and pressed her lips to his, cutting him off. There was no hesitancy on her part. She leaned in and meshed her mouth with his, hard and demanding and full of her yearning.

He could do nothing less than meet her kiss for kiss, bending in and mingling his mouth with hers in return, letting her lead as desire rushed in to swamp him, crashing over him and drowning him all in one move.

With each touch of his lips to hers, he wanted her to know how much he loved her. He adored everything about her and knew that if he searched the whole world over, he would never find another woman who fit with him the way Emberly did.

The truth was, he had searched near and far for the right woman, and he had failed at every turn . . . until now. She was beyond perfect for him, and he could not let her get away. He had to marry her.

He was getting ahead of himself. After all, he had just declared his love to her. He could not bring up marriage and scare her away.

Her arms slid up to behind his neck, and in the same motion, she drew closer so that her body was pressed against his. At the warmth and softness and curves, a moan reverberated in his throat, and he dropped his hands, sliding his arms around her so that he could hold her more fully.

He rested his hands at the small of her back and had to stop himself from letting his hands roam free. He loved her enough that he did not want to take advantage of their being stranded together and stuck in the cabin. He needed to end the kiss before it awoke in him strong desires that should stay dormant for the night.

With a self-control he'd cultivated over the years, he gentled his mouth against hers, tasting her sweetness slowly and languidly, hungry for all of her but reminding himself that she was so much more than her body and kisses, and she deserved to be cherished.

As he ended the kiss, he shifted his mouth to her forehead and pressed a kiss there. Her arms around him only tightened. That was a good sign, was it not? She had not only initiated the kiss, but she also did not want it to end.

"I love you, darling," he whispered before kissing her forehead again.

Her fingers fisted in his shirt at his back.

A hot spear sliced into his gut. Oh yes, the desire between them was certainly strong.

"Max," she whispered, then she buried her face against his chest. "What is happening here between us?"

Was she worried that he would pressure her for more tonight?

He took a step back so that he could look down into her face.

Her cheeks were flushed, her lashes halfway down, and her lips still swollen.

Once again heat seared him, and he couldn't keep from tightening his grip on her hips. He wanted to pull her flush again and ravage her lips with another kiss. She was so beautiful, and more so because of all the things he loved about her.

"We shared a kiss," he whispered, keeping her at arm's length. "And that is all we shall share tonight. I vow it."

Her eyes widened, revealing the rich, silky brown that had the power to undo him and make him forget about everything else. "But what does the kiss mean to you? What can it mean? I just don't know where this can go."

"What does it mean to me? Where can it go?" Should he be completely honest with her, even if his honesty scared her away?

"We live in two different worlds," she continued, "have two different lives—"

"I want to marry you."

Another happy tsk came from the other side of the wall. Apparently, Braun approved of his bumbling efforts at winning Emberly.

Emberly, on the other hand, was studying his face again, this time with eyes narrowing in disbelief. She gave a huff, then pushed at his chest and took a large step back. "Don't say that, Max."

"That I want to marry you?"

She moved farther away. "You can't say that."

"Whyever not?"

"Because it's not true and would never happen."

"It certainly is true, and I can marry whomever I wish."

She bumped into the couch and plopped down. "What about Sarah?"

"I have never loved her."

"I thought you wanted to learn to be love-crazy so you could win her."

"You are the only one I want to be love-crazy with."

She palmed her head as though she could not quite believe what he was saying.

He had to make it very clear that his intention to marry her was genuine. He crossed to her, lowered himself to one knee in front of her, and then reached for her hand. "Please do me the honor of becoming my wife."

15

Was she dreaming?

Max had told her he loved her. Twice. Now he was down on one knee proposing marriage to her.

This was crazy. Wasn't it?

Even if it was crazy, it was the kind of love-crazy she'd always witnessed in her family, the kind she'd always longed for but never believed possible.

His handsome features were taut with earnestness, and his eyes were bright and filled with hope.

They'd just shared an amazing kiss—the kind of kiss she would never forget, not even if she lived a hundred years. It was a kiss that she hadn't wanted to end, one that had whisked her off her feet and deposited her on the clouds so that she'd been floating in pure bliss.

His lips . . . his mouth . . .

Her gaze dropped to his lips and mouth—so firm, so determined, so sensual. He was an amazing kisser, and she wanted to kiss him again right now.

In fact, she wanted to answer his proposal the same way she'd answered his declaration of love—with a kiss. Was it a way to avoid responding? Or was it her way of saying yes? She wasn't quite sure.

But he was waiting for a real answer this time, and she had to say something. "Max, I want to say yes . . . because I think I'm falling in love with you too . . ."

He expelled a tight breath at the same time as a smile broke free—one of his genuine smiles that made his face irresistibly charming.

"But . . ." she quickly continued, "I don't want to rush things."

"And I do not wish to pressure you." He caressed her hand. "You do not need to answer me now about marriage. I just want you to know I am serious about us and covet having a future together."

She could see the truth of his statement in his eyes. He wasn't saying this to get something from her or to lead her on. He truly wanted to be with her.

Deep inside, she knew she wanted to be with him too. Even though their predicament was dangerous, she was relishing every extra moment they'd been given. Tomorrow would come too soon, and the prospect of his leaving was only getting harder to think about.

How had she fallen for him this quickly? How was it possible she was in love with him? Because now that she'd confessed her love for him aloud, she realized she felt that love deep inside, all the way to her bones.

Maybe she was experiencing the McQuaid legacy of love after all.

She wasn't sure, but she did know she wanted to talk more before agreeing to marry him. She supposed she was too much of a planner, too detail-oriented, too calculating to simply throw away all caution and agree to marry him without any discussion on how it would all work.

She patted the spot beside her. "Can we discuss this more? There are so many logistics we need to think about."

He rose and then lowered himself onto the couch, keeping several inches between them—several inches too much.

Now that they'd kissed and declared their love and talked about marriage, she wanted to be close to him, to curl up against him and have him hold her. She'd kept up her guard, hadn't let herself dream of having more with him, had tried to remain realistic about them. But now . . . she couldn't stop her heart from wanting to have everything. Her pulse was beating hard with a need for him that had been unleashed and could no longer be contained.

"You can sit closer and hold me," she whispered.

He hesitated.

"I promise I'll behave," she teased as she walked two

fingers up his arm in a pretend enticement.

"I am more concerned about my own ability to *behave* than yours." He slanted a sideways look at her—a short one, but long enough for her to see the heat in his gaze and to know her presence affected him.

She dropped her fingers from his arm and reached for his hand instead. As her fingers wound around his, he flipped his hand over and intertwined their fingers securely, resting their hands on the couch in the space that separated them.

They were both quiet. She was relishing his touch, the strength of his hold, the possessive curl of his fingers. Was she really sitting next to him, holding his hand? A thrill whispered through her—a thrill that made her almost lightheaded.

After the breakup with Ryan and the past year of feeling rejected, she had never imagined she would fall in love this way.

"A marriage to a prince such as myself would come with challenges," he said after a moment. "I would wish to spare you as many of those challenges as possible, but I am afraid some are unavoidable."

"I'm not afraid of challenges."

He gave her a small smile. "That is true. You are a strong woman."

"Be honest with me, Max." Not that his honesty would change her feelings for him. But she did need to know what she might be getting herself into if she agreed to marry him. "What will be some of the hardest parts about being your wife?"

"Being constantly in the spotlight and having the paparazzi interested and prying into your personal life."

She'd witnessed her brother Brock going through all of that. It hadn't always been easy for him, especially when unfair and untrue rumors circulated about him. But he'd learned how to handle the pressure. "I'm not worried about the spotlight or paparazzi."

"It can be difficult and daunting during those times we wish for privacy and instead our secrets are made public."

"Like when you broke up with Sarah?"

"Yes. The media will turn everything into a sensationalized story. As a result, it puts a great deal of pressure upon everyone."

"I'm sorry that you were feeling so much pressure." She could only imagine that had been part of the pressure he'd been trying to avoid when he'd arrived at the ranch. She brushed her fingers over his. "What else will be hard about being your wife?"

"My wife will also have certain responsibilities, public appearances, and traditions and customs to uphold."

"Like what?"

They settled into the sofa, and he shared about what she would experience as a princess married to him and then what she could expect if she became queen someday. The duties sounded a lot like what she was already doing as an event manager, except on a larger scale in helping to coordinate parties and events for the royal household, attending charities and benefits, representing the family's interests, and caring about the people of the nation.

Max also talked about growing up as a prince. Although he'd already told her about his family and his brothers, this time he opened up about the trials of being the heir apparent. He was honest about the difficulties as well as the benefits of his life, and he didn't gloss over the many challenges he would face in the years to come in a changing and sometimes volatile world.

Throughout their discussion, it was easy to see how seriously he took his role, how passionate he was about his position, and how he'd prepared for years to take over his father's duties. He would need to shoulder a heavy load; the responsibilities would be great and the pressure immense. But Max had proven to be a strong and determined man, and she had no doubt he would handle everything well.

She was full of questions about what his life was really like, where he lived, and what his duties as prince were. She admitted she'd googled him to find out more information and had found his picture with more women than she could count. He confessed to having a wild period of his life when he was at the university and for a while after that.

Although she was a little jealous of all the women he'd known, he assured her that none of them had mattered, that he'd never felt for them anything like what he felt for her. The relationships had been shallow and had lacked substance compared to the one with her, which was mature and deep and real.

At some point late in the night, Max got up to add more wood to the stove while the storm continued to howl through the cracks and rattle the windows and roof. She had a feeling things were only getting worse with the storm rather than better, but she tried not to worry about it. Instead, she soaked in every minute of holding Max's hand beside him on the couch and talking about everything.

The second time Max got up, dawn was only an hour or two away, and she couldn't keep her eyes open any longer. When Max sat back down, she curled up next to him, put the blanket over both of them, then laid her head on his shoulder. Within seconds, she was asleep.

She wasn't sure how long she drifted off. When she stirred later, she realized that somehow she and Max had ended up lying beside each other. He had his back against the cushions, and she had her back against him, and both of their heads were on the same couch pillow. His arms surrounded her and held her securely, his hands together across her stomach. The blanket covered mostly her, but her warmth came from him and his encompassing hold.

She didn't want to wake up, wanted to go back to sleep this way and never have to get up from the couch again, so that she could lie in his arms forever.

Could she really allow herself to dream about waking up with him every morning? Was that really a possibility? Max had seemed to think so. He'd made it clear she was special and that he'd never loved or wanted to marry a woman the way he did her.

She released a contented sigh.

"Are you awake, darling?" came his whisper against her hair.

"No. I'm asleep and plan to stay that way for a while."

He chuckled softly.

She loved the rumble against her back, the strength of his arms around her, and the pressure of his long legs against hers. She shifted backward and snuggled into him even more.

At the movement, his arms tightened, and he bent and pressed a kiss to her head, a long and hard one that contained all of the passion he was obviously holding back.

Heat swirled languidly inside her. But more than the heat, a deep sense of appreciation swelled up into her throat, choking her with sudden emotion. This man was truly honorable. He'd vowed that nothing would happen except that kiss they'd shared last night, and he'd kept his promise. That's the kind of man Max was—a man of strength, character, and the highest caliber.

There was no sense in playing any games with herself or with him. She may as well be completely honest. She loved him, and she wanted to marry him. No amount of time would change that. Not a few weeks or a few months. So why not admit it now?

"Max?" she whispered.

"Yes, darling." He pressed another kiss to the back of her head, this one gentler.

"I know I love you."

His whole body stilled. "Truly?"

"And I do want to marry you, because I can't bear the thought of living without you."

This time he breathed out what sounded like relief. "Hearing you say so makes me a very happy man, the happiest ever."

She couldn't hold back a smile of her own happiness. "You know what would make me happy right now?"

"What?"

"If you kissed me again." Her words were bold, but she'd been thinking about their kiss for hours, and her craving for another was only growing.

"I vowed I would not kiss you again." His voice turned husky. "Believe me, I have worked incredibly hard to keep my vow. I had to exert herculean strength in order to resist the temptation of turning you over and kissing you senseless."

Sweet pleasure washed over her at his words, and she closed her eyes again to bask in the beauty of the moment with him. "You said you wouldn't kiss me again last night. But it's morning now."

"You have an excellent point."

"It's brilliant."

"Very much so." He shifted and she found herself slipping down so that she was on her back, peering up at him. He was still sideways beside her, one arm across her stomach and the other propping himself up.

Max had extinguished the lantern above the table long ago to conserve oil, but the glow from the stove provided enough light that she could see his starkly handsome face with his scruffy cheeks, his long nose, and his carved jaw covered in his short beard. He looked good enough to kiss all over.

But no, she wouldn't give in to that desire. She couldn't. That would be too much. But they could share one more reasonable kiss. There wouldn't be anything wrong with that.

"Kiss me," she whispered again, this time arching up.

Releasing a hungry growl, he bent down, and in the next instant, his mouth was upon hers. He held nothing back, devouring her with a passion that showed just how powerful, formidable, and commanding he really was.

She loved knowing he was one of the most influential

men in the world and that he was kissing her like she was his greatest treasure and possession. She loved that at the same time as he was forceful, he was equally restrained and in control of himself. In fact, as he lifted a hand to her cheek and caressed her, the slight tremor told her how much it was costing him to hold himself back.

As he leaned in further, his body grazed hers. He was so solid and strong. She wanted to wrap both arms around him and drag him down on top of her. She craved more of him, more connections, more of his touching.

It would be all too easy to get carried away and let the kissing stir up more passion that needed to remain banked for now, especially since they had so many arrangements yet to make for their relationship before they could actually be together. How soon could they set a wedding date? And how long would it actually take to plan a wedding of the caliber his family would require? Where would they get married? His country or hers? And who would they invite?

The questions tumbled through her, and she pulled away from the kiss.

He immediately lifted his head away, giving her space and not trying to continue the kiss, even though his breathing was labored and his hand on her stomach was taut.

He didn't say anything for a moment, almost as if he was trying to regain control over himself first.

She needed to find her equilibrium again too, because kissing him shook her to the core and made her dizzy with need.

"What is wrong, darling?" His voice was low and filled with both desire and tenderness.

"I was just thinking of the wedding."

"And . . . ?"

He was learning to read her well, and she liked that. "And I guess I'm scared."

"Of what?"

"That I'll make mistakes and upset your family or mine."

He was quiet for several heartbeats. "Then let us not have a wedding. Instead, we shall elope."

"Elope?"

"Yes, we shall get married privately, then tell everyone after the fact."

She smiled. "I know what eloping is. I just hadn't expected you to suggest it."

"Why not?"

"As a prince, wouldn't everyone be excited to know you're engaged and hope to see your wedding ceremony, sort of like everyone wanted to watch Kate marry Prince William?"

His hand was still resting on her stomach, but some of the tension had eased from his hold. "Joseph can give the public the royal wedding they crave."

She'd learned that Joseph was his youngest brother and was marrying a titled English woman later in the year. It would apparently be a big occasion because Joseph's fiancée's family was very wealthy and liked to show off their money.

Max's brow furrowed, and he removed his hand from her stomach to trace a line down her cheek. "Forgive me. I would not prevent you from having a lovely wedding if that is what your heart desires."

She laughed lightly. "Oh, Max. After all you've learned about me, do I strike you as the type of woman who wants a *lovely wedding*?"

"Not necessarily. But some women do have their hearts set on having the whole enormous occasion."

"Not me. I don't have any desire to plan a big wedding, maybe because I plan events for a living."

"If you truly want a wedding of any size, we shall hire a wedding coordinator."

She couldn't believe she was here beside Max and having this kind of conversation. What would her family say? Her brothers? "Maybe we should elope." She was only half teasing him back. "Then we won't have to worry about my brothers interfering."

"I suppose they will object to how fast we became engaged?"

"Oh yeah. No question about it."

"Tyler will likely be livid."

"*All* of them will object, and they'll try to scold me into doing what they think is best."

Max's fingers slipped down to her neck and made a trail behind her ear to her collarbone. Every single movement was making her less coherent and more in need of another kiss.

A worry line formed in Max's forehead, and he dropped his hand away from her. "I do not wish to lose you, Emberly."

"You won't."

"But your brothers are important to you, and they have a great deal of influence over you. What if they try to convince you to stay away from me?"

"I won't let them." But could she really guarantee that her brothers would leave her alone once she declared to them that she loved Max? Maybe it was past time to stand up to them and show them that she wasn't the weak, fragile college dropout they thought she was. Maybe it was time to show everyone that she was strong enough and old enough to make her own decisions, especially when it came to love and marriage.

"I can help you withstand their influence while I am here. But what about when I leave, as I must do soon?"

"I'll go with you." The words slipped out before she could stop them. She wasn't normally so rash, but she knew deep inside that she was ready for a change, ready to start a new chapter in her life, ready for new adventures.

"Truly?" Did his voice contain a hint of excitement?

"Yes, truly."

"Will you consider eloping and returning with me to my country as my wife?"

16

Max could hardly breathe. Stretched out on the couch beside Emberly, he had already been having difficulty because the kiss had taken his breath away.

Now, as he waited for her response to whether she would elope and return with him to his country, his lungs failed to work once more.

"So you're serious about eloping?" she asked quietly, her voice contemplative.

"I am extremely serious. This is not the first time I have longed to simply elope with you."

Her eyes widened. "Really? When?"

"At the rodeo a few days ago." He could not recall at the moment why he had considered the option, only that it had crossed his mind. "Does that bother you?"

"It flatters me that you were already interested in marrying me then."

"I have been interested in you much longer than

that." His voice was gravelly.

A smile tugged at her lips. "Have you now?"

"I most certainly have." He had an overwhelming desire to swoop down and kiss those lips again. But he was afraid of what might happen if he gave way to more kisses. He had been noble thus far, and he wanted to continue to be noble in his aspirations toward her. But he was not a saint, and she was an exceptionally beautiful and vivacious woman who had captured his heart, soul, and body.

"But why, Max?" She studied his face, obviously seeking the truth. "Why elope?"

He wanted to make sure he spoke his best arguments to convince her. So for a long moment, he attempted to put together his thoughts while the blowing of the wind against the cabin filled the silence. "For one," he finally said, "I am not getting any younger, and I would like to have as much time as possible with you."

She cocked her head in that sassy way he liked. "It's not like you have one foot in the grave."

"No, but I have waited a long time to get married, and now that I have found you, the one I love, I do not wish to waste a single moment more of my life without you."

She smiled again, this time more fully. "I like that reason."

"Good." He smiled in return. "Two, as we discussed,

I would like to avoid opposition from your family. But I would also like to avoid it from mine as well."

Her smile fell away. "Will they oppose you marrying me? Of course your father will. If he disapproved of Ava, then he will disapprove of me too."

He wished he could tell her their relationship would be well received, but that was not the case. "The precedent does not give the king the right to choose my wife, but tradition stipulates he should approve of the woman."

"And if you elope, he won't be able to approve."

"Neither will he be able to disapprove."

Emberly shook her head, then scrambled to sit up. "Well, we both know he won't like me, and I don't want to be the source of conflict between the two of you."

Max pushed himself up so that he was sitting beside her. He would not let his father ruin his chance with Emberly. Not now and not ever. He pressed his shoulders back and then took Emberly's hands in his. "My father lost his right to approve of my wife when he interfered with Ava and bribed her father to find someone else for her."

"I doubt he would be able to bribe my dad."

"I concur." T.W. didn't seem like the type of man who would be easily swayed away from something once he had made up his mind. At least, Max hoped the man had been serious in his statement that Emberly was perfect for him. "I shall not let him do anything to undermine my relationship with you. If we elope, then he cannot do anything but accept my choice."

"He can't make you divorce me or give me an annulment?"

"No, he does not have the authority to dictate what I do."

Again, Emberly fell silent, and no doubt she was contemplating all he had spoken.

"I hope you know that while I love my father, I long ago stopped living to please him, particularly in matrimonial matters."

"I think I understand." She stared at her hands twisting the blanket in her lap. "Even so, I don't want your father to hate me."

"I also do not wish for your brothers to hate me." He spoke gently but firmly. "I do hope that eventually they will accept me. However, I shall not let their view influence my decision to marry you."

She turned her big brown eyes upon him. Every time she looked at him so openly and without any pretense, he fell more in love with her for accepting him as a regular person and not fixating on his being a prince.

"Can you do the same with my father? Can you keep him from influencing your decision to marry me?"

"I think I can." She reached for his hand.

Her fingers were cold, and he took both of her hands

and pressed them between his to offer her warmth.

She didn't resist and instead shifted closer to him. "I try not to worry about what people think about me for the most part. But this is your father we're talking about. The king of your country."

"I have the feeling he will learn to love you, especially once he gets to know you the same way I have."

"And your mother?"

"My mother is a very strong woman, not unlike you. She is also very reasonable, and I do think she will accept you and be happy for me, for us."

He situated himself more comfortably and pulled Emberly into the crook of his arm, making sure the blanket was tucked around her. They talked until dawn light began to fill the cabin, more about their future together, where they would live, and what they would do.

"I should like to cut my hours back at the bank," he said as he rose to add more fuel to the fire. "I shall delegate more responsibility to other capable workers." The more he'd done so on this trip, the more he'd been able to let go of the feeling that so much rested on his shoulders. It really didn't. The bank operations had gone on just fine without him.

Besides, was it possible he'd turned to his work at the bank in an effort to fill the loneliness in his life? That he had been using work to meet a need that could only truly be met by people he loved? 'Twas a possibility he needed to ponder.

"If you work less"—she stood and stretched—"then you'll have time to be my personal tour guide there the same way I was for you here."

"Yes, I shall be your personal guide, just as you were for me. I shall show you Karltenberg and everything about it and my country." They could visit all his family's estates and experience the things he loved about each place.

"Then I'll expect a lot of one-on-one time." She tossed him a sassy look.

"One-on-one time?" His blood heated just thinking about all the one-on-one time he planned to have with her. "Of course. I would not have it any other way."

From the other room, Braun tsked loudly enough for Max to know he was awake and once again listening to his conversation with Emberly.

Max had heard Winzig stirring in the bedroom a short while ago and guessed his bodyguard would be anxious to get him to safety at first light. The question that had been nagging Max all night was whether they would be able to go anywhere with the way the wind was still blowing. He suspected the snow had finally stopped, but now the problem would be the drifting and the cold.

If the conditions were impassable or dangerous, would they have no choice but to stay? If they were trapped, the situation could grow precarious. Would they have enough fuel and food for four people? Max's stomach was already gnawing after their sparse supper the previous evening, involving leftovers from their lunch coupled with canned food from the cabin's pantry.

Winzig stepped out of the bedroom, rubbing his hands together and blowing into them for warmth. The bedroom likely hadn't stayed as warm as the main room, which was not entirely warm anymore either, likely because of the dropping temperature outside.

While Winzig lit the lantern, Emberly began making the coffee. They were joined shortly by Braun, who was also in need of warming up. As they sipped coffee, they discussed the situation and decided that when they had full daylight, they would go out and investigate the landscape and weather and assess whether leaving was possible.

Their phone batteries were all growing low, and they had no way to charge them. So they decided to turn them off to conserve the little battery they did have left.

When dawn turned into full daylight, they donned their outer gear and ventured outside. Although Max wanted to shelter Emberly and protect her and make her stay inside where she would be warm and dry, he also loved her feistiness and desire to be a part of the solution. Besides, she was the most experienced of them in the mountains and knew the area the best.

The conditions were worse than they'd anticipated. The wind was still gusting, but the snow seemed to have stopped falling for the most part. The drifts in some places were more than a meter high, but it was difficult to estimate exactly how much had accumulated. They were fortunate the cabin had a front porch that had prevented the drifts from trapping them in the cabin.

As it was, the sharp drop in the temperature seemed to be their greatest threat. They worked together to bring in more wood from a pile at the back of the cabin that was still mostly dry. They also brought in a large pan of snow to melt and use for cooking and drinking. Then they settled back into the cabin and waited for the conditions to improve.

Emberly suggested conserving the oil in the lantern as well as rationing their food. Although she did not expound, Max could easily assess that she was taking the precautions because she, too, expected they may not be able to leave anytime soon.

When he suggested that her family would surely send out a search party, she shook her head gravely and explained that no one would be able to travel up to the cabin by foot, not without great peril. And until the wind abated, not even her brother Kade in his helicopter would be able to fly out.

Whatever might happen, all that really mattered to Max was that he was with Emberly and would hopefully never have to leave her again.

17

"We'll find a way down the mountain." Emberly tried to keep a reassuring tone as she took a sip of her coffee. The afternoon was passing and so were their chances of leaving that day.

She was tucked against Max's side as they sat beside each other on a bench at the table. With Braun and Winzig having overheard her and Max's conversation last night when they'd declared their love to each other, they were doing nothing now to hide their affection. What was the point?

Max rubbed her arm over the blanket he'd draped on top of her. "Perhaps tomorrow the wind will be gone, and sunshine will take its place."

"It's possible." Even if the sunshine came out and began to melt the snow, would they be able to make it back on snowmobiles? The snow might be too deep and the risk of avalanches too great.

At this point, they just had to wait. And even though they were all trying to have positive attitudes, she could sense the men's constant worry about the situation.

"Look at the bright side," she added as she laid her head on Max's arm and snuggled into him. "We get to be together a few extra days."

"Remember, darling." Max paused in his shuffling of the deck of cards for another game of solitaire. "We decided we would get married and that you would return with me to Karltenberg."

Yes, that's what they had talked about. But could she really do it? Last night in the dark, beside him on the couch after sharing kisses, the choices had all seemed so much easier than now by the light of day, when her mind was clearer.

As if sensing her hesitancy, Max set aside the deck of cards.

Across the table, Braun paused in his writing of numbers in a sudoku book he'd found on the game shelf. At the front window, Winzig shifted in their direction. Neither man seemed surprised by Max's news. Yet they were clearly waiting for him to say more.

Max, on the other hand, seemed to be waiting for her to agree with him.

Could she?

She wanted to be with Max, but the doubts came rushing back—this was too soon, they'd only just met, they were so different, and family might not approve. Also, what about her job? She couldn't just leave without helping find a replacement.

What about being so far away from her dad when he was still recovering? While his cancer was in remission, there was always the chance it could come back. And everyone knew his life expectancy was still uncertain.

Would she really be able to fit into Max's world? He had assured her she would learn everything quickly and that he would be by her side to help her, but what if she embarrassed him enough that his people rejected her?

She loved Max. That had become very obvious. But she wasn't sure she should rush into marrying him.

Braun laid the pencil down on the open sudoku book. "Congratulations are in order."

"Yes." Max's probing gaze held hers. "I was able to convince Emberly to marry me. I think."

"Of course I'm marrying you." She squeezed his arm tighter, wanting to reassure him. "But we didn't really decide when."

"I would like to do so as soon as possible," Max stated firmly.

"But shouldn't I give my two weeks' notice at work?"

"I imagine you could still do quite a bit of your work remotely, could you not?"

"I suppose so." Many of the details of her event planning could be done anywhere as long as she had her laptop.

"Is something else bothering you?" he asked gently, his silvery-green eyes filling with tenderness.

"I'm just nervous, that's all." She already knew she needed to get married to him soon so that neither of their families would try to prevent the marriage. But how soon?

Braun's gaze was bouncing back and forth between them. "You do not need to be nervous with His Royal Highness. Max has been in love with you from almost the moment he laid eyes on you."

She bumped her shoulder against Max's. "Is that right?"

"It is," Braun interjected emphatically before Max could get a word in. "I have never seen Max react so strongly to one woman. He could not get enough of you. He still obviously cannot."

She smiled. "I love hearing the inside scoop."

Max ducked his head, his gaze turning sheepish. "I cannot deny Braun."

Her heart warmed at his admission.

Braun tapped his pencil on the table. "If you would like to get married before returning to Karltenberg, I could offer you my services as an officiant."

"You are an officiant?" Max quirked his brow at Braun.

"Yes, I have my license as a registrar of vital statistics."

"Of course you do." Max's charming grin made an appearance. "Why does that not surprise me?"

Braun tsked. "It should not. Being a registrar is a perfectly acceptable hobby."

The man was one of the most eccentric people she'd ever met, but she liked him more for it. "So, does being a registrar mean you have the power to perform a wedding?"

"I have the legal authority, yes, and have married two couples—my cousin and his wife, along with a friend from university."

"What else should I know about you, Braun?" Max's voice held a note of teasing.

"I am also a licensed scuba-diving instructor."

Max nodded. "Yes, I was aware of that."

But why? Did Karltenberg even have places to scuba dive?

Emberly wasn't sure what Braun's scuba diving had to do with being a registrar who could marry people—maybe the licensed part? Whatever the case, Braun was proving to be a man of many talents.

"I could marry you today if I so choose," Braun continued with all seriousness.

"Today?" Max's grip around Emberly tightened.

"Yes, if you want to get married today, I could perform the ceremony in an official capacity."

Max pushed their bench back from the table, released her, and stood. He was staring at Braun, his humor now gone, his expression serious. "Do not jest with me, Braun."

Braun stood now too. "Have I ever jested with you, Your Highness?"

Max held Braun's gaze. "I suppose you have not."

"I would not start now about such a serious matter."

The cabin grew suddenly silent. Or maybe Emberly's heart and lungs had ceased to function. Was Max really considering having Braun marry them today? And if so, would she agree to it?

As if hearing her silent questions, Max turned to her, his eyes shining with hope and love—the kind of hope and love she'd seen in her dad's eyes many times over the years when he'd looked at Mom.

Was Max love-crazy for her? He was sure making her feel like she was the most important person in his life and all that really mattered to him.

A thrill wound through her, tingling down to her toes. She'd never thought she could have the McQuaid legacy of love, had always believed she would have to settle for a marriage and a man who would come close but never quite be able to live up to her family's standards.

It looked like she was wrong. She and Max were experiencing something powerful—a fast, furious, and forever love.

"What do you think, Emberly?" Max asked softly. "Should we get married today?"

Should they get married today? At this moment, all the reasons to say no to Max seemed to fade away and were no longer important. It didn't matter what anyone else would say or think. He was more important than any of her excuses. Their love was more valuable than anything else. And their being together was essential.

A swell of love rose inside her so swiftly and powerfully that she closed the gap between them, wrapped her arms around him, and met Max's gaze again. "I'm willing if you are."

He bent in and touched his lips to hers in a sweet kiss that was over before it could begin. "I am more than willing. I can think of nothing else I want more."

18

He was getting married. After so many years of searching and trying and failing, how had this happened so swiftly and with such certainty?

With Winzig standing beside him as a witness, Max faced Emberly, holding both of her hands as she finished stating her vows. His chest ached with all the love he felt for her. It simply could not be contained inside him.

"Your turn, Your Highness," Braun said as he stood in front of them, attempting to look stately. But having no way to groom himself, he was decidedly rumpled with his hair messy, his beard no longer neatly trimmed, and his clothing wrinkled.

Max was curious to know how Braun could recite the order verbatim. Perhaps he had memorized the ceremony when he'd performed his previous marriage ceremonies. Whatever the case, Max was grateful for Braun's many talents.

Max repeated the words, holding Emberly's gaze and hoping she could see that he meant every single one. "I Nikolaus Constantin Maximillian Karltenberg take you, Emberly McQuaid, to be my wedded wife, to have and to hold from this day forward, for better, for worse, for richer, for poorer, in sickness and in health, to love and to cherish till death us do part, according to God's holy will."

He would love and cherish her with every breath he had. He brought her hand up to his lips and placed a kiss on her knuckles. "I love you, darling."

Braun shook his head. "That is not part of the ceremony, Your Highness."

"It should be. I would like it to be."

Braun pursed his lips.

But as Emberly's eyes crinkled at the corners with the beginning of a smile, Max persisted. "In fact, I would like to be able to express my love to my bride whenever it suits me."

"You cannot—"

Max cut Braun off with one of his most severe glares, one that demanded acquiescence as his superior. Max was not above using his royal privileges to get what he wanted from time to time. At the moment, he needed to assure Emberly how much he loved her, needed her to know so that she had no reservations about what they were doing.

He had witnessed her silent doubts over the past few

hours since Braun had first offered to marry them. Of course, Max had wanted to have the ceremony right away and not give her any time to overthink their relationship and change her mind.

But they had agreed they would make the most of the remaining hours of daylight, especially because the wind had grown calmer. They had attempted to climb to the highest spot near the cabin, hoping to get a cell phone connection. The way up had been precarious, and he and Emberly had not gone far before turning back.

They had also begun shoveling a path to the nearby lake. Emberly indicated that they could ice-fish there if necessary. What she left unsaid was that they might run out of food and need the sustenance.

When they had finally been too frozen to remain outside any longer, they had all retreated into the cabin and locked themselves away for another night. Emberly had said she needed a little time to prepare for the wedding and had gone into the bedroom, where she had styled her hair as best she could, pulling a few strands up and leaving the rest down. He regretted that she did not have an elegant dress to change into, that she had only the jeans and sweater she'd worn yesterday.

However, she was more than stunning, especially because her eyes shone with love for him, her expression was sincere, and her lips were curved into a small smile.

"I love you, darling," he said again, and this time

followed his declaration by bending down and touching his lips to hers.

Her mouth was absolutely delectable, tasting sweet and fresh. Her lips always responded to his so eagerly, so willingly, so passionately. Every time he kissed her, he told himself the kiss would sate his hunger for her, that he would be fulfilled. But the opposite seemed to be happening. Every time he touched her lips, he only wanted to taste her again and craved her even more.

Braun cleared his throat obnoxiously.

Emberly was the one to pull back, nibbling at her lip and attempting not to smile and so irritate Braun even more.

"Let us pray." Braun bowed his head, and Winzig followed suit.

Emberly closed her eyes, and Max's heartbeat sped with the wonder that she was his wife.

"Eternal God, Our Creator and Redeemer. Just as you gladdened the wedding at Cana in Galilee by the presence of your Son, so gladden this wedding with your presence now."

Emberly opened one eye and caught Max staring. She immediately smiled, clearly entertained by Braun's ability to perform the ceremony so perfectly. At least no one could accuse them of not having a traditional wedding, including a short sermon that Braun had already delivered as well as a recitation of 1 Corinthians 13.

As Braun made the sign of the cross and opened his eyes, he frowned at the sight of the two of them staring at each other. "Since we have no rings, I shall skip ahead to the benediction."

"The ring that is set aside for my bride is a family heirloom." Max squeezed Emberly's hand. "I shall give it to you once we are at the palace in Vollenstadt."

"I'd like to give you a wedding ring too."

"There is a traditional ring for the groom as well."

"I want to give you one that comes from me, from my heart."

At her words, he wanted to bend down and kiss her again. But with the way Braun was frowning, he merely nodded. "Of course. I shall treasure such a gift from you."

"Dearly loved." Braun's voice rose several decibels. "By their promises before God and this assembly, Nikolaus Constantin Maximillian and Emberly have joined themselves as husband and wife. What God has joined together, let no one separate."

Husband and wife. They were officially married.

"Thanks be to God." Braun spoke solemnly. "Amen."

"Amen," Emberly whispered.

"I now pronounce that you are husband and wife." Braun took a step back and folded his hands together as though he was closing the order of service.

Max waited.

Braun raised a brow.

"You are forgetting something."

"No, I am not."

"Yes, you are. You have yet to say that I may kiss my wife."

"Your Highness, clearly you do not need my permission for doing so since you have already been taking liberties all throughout the ceremony."

Emberly chuckled.

"You are not wrong, Braun. But please. Could you humor me and say the words?"

"That will be no trouble, Your Highness, since I am accustomed to humoring you." Braun cleared his throat. "I now present you as husband and wife. You may kiss your bride."

Max reached for Emberly, and she came to him eagerly, falling against him. He wrapped one hand around her, then dipped her backward and gave her another kiss, this one full of tenderness and desire and promise for the future.

As they straightened, she laughed with delight, a laugh that filled his heart with the assurance he had done the right thing in marrying this woman as hastily as he could so that she couldn't slip from his grasp the same way Ava had. Now she was his, and no one could change that fact, not even his father.

After the wedding was done, they opened the bottle of wine in the hutch and ate the four cookies they had saved from their lunch yesterday. Braun insisted on giving a toast and rambled for a good five minutes, but it was full of his loyalty and love for Max. When he finished, he cajoled Winzig into giving a toast too, which lasted all of three seconds: "Long live the prince and his princess."

Finally, with a loud yawn, Braun stood and stretched. "It has been an exhausting day, and Winzig and I can barely keep our eyes open."

Winzig had just finished his glass of wine and was wide-eyed. He raised his brow at Braun.

Braun fluttered his hands. "Come on with you now. Off to bed you go."

Winzig rose reluctantly.

It was rather early to retire, especially because the day had not been exhausting in the least, since they had sat around for most of it and not exerted themselves much.

As Braun hustled Winzig into the bedroom, he paused in the doorway. "Enjoy your night, Your Highness. I promise we shall close our ears and allow you to have all the privacy you need with your new bride."

Beside him, Emberly stiffened, clearly catching Braun's insinuation that they would spend the night together consummating their marriage. Braun was only suggesting something that was entirely appropriate and even necessary for a royal marriage such as his.

But ... as much as Max desired Emberly and would take great pleasure in kissing her all night long, he refused to subject her to a romp on the couch in a musty cabin with his people on the other side of a paper-thin wall. He cared about her too much and wanted their first time together as man and wife to be special so that he could properly convey just how much he adored her.

He could not say so to Emberly at the moment, but as soon as they were alone, he would share his thoughts on the matter and assure her that he would not pressure her now or anytime.

19

With Braun's comments still hanging in the air, Emberly was squirming as she settled onto the couch, even though she didn't normally embarrass easily.

Of course, Max didn't seem bothered at all as he added wood to the fire.

He was her husband. How wild was that?

He'd been so doting and sweet all throughout the wedding ceremony, reassuring her of how much he loved her and wanting to kiss her frequently. She'd loved every moment.

While he wasn't a McQuaid and would never be exactly like Dad in his love for Mom, Max was proving himself to be a man who wanted to love deeply and passionately and intentionally. Maybe he was that way because of his age and maturity. Maybe he was that way because of all he'd learned from previous failed relationships. Maybe he was that way because he was taking seriously the need to be love-crazy.

Whatever it was, she had no regrets about marrying him so quickly and pledging her life to him. He was the kind of man she'd never believed she'd ever find. And now he was hers.

She could admit, even after their conversations, that she was still nervous about him being royalty. If she'd been able to choose who he was, she wouldn't have picked him being a prince. Even the CEO of the world's richest bank was a bit much for a woman like her. But his training to be a prince and an investment banker had shaped him into the man she'd fallen in love with, so she couldn't separate out those things about him, not when they were important to him.

Instead, she would have to work at accepting who he was and all that entailed. Her own mom had done that when she'd married into the McQuaid ranch. She'd started a new life as a cowgirl and rancher's wife, and she'd eventually adjusted.

Emberly wanted to adjust too. But she also didn't want her identity to disappear. She liked her family's heritage and history. She was proud of all that her ancestors had accomplished, and she knew she would need to find ways to stay connected to her family and her past, even though she was moving away.

Regardless of what her new life would bring, nothing else really mattered as long as she was with Max. Not only was there so much substance already to their relationship, but the chemistry between them was flaming hot and had only been growing hotter all day.

At the moment, it flickered in the air, shooting sparks over her and heating her. She wanted to be close to him and hold him and not have to ignore her attraction to him any longer. But the cabin and the situation weren't very romantic, not with two other grown men there.

Max closed the stove, then straightened, the glow from the fire outlining his magnificent body—his long legs, lean torso, and handsome face. He held himself with such confidence and determination, as if he could battle the whole world and remain strong.

Love for him rushed through her like the gusts of wind that had blown against the mountainside all day. She held out a hand, beckoning him closer.

He didn't move and instead watched her, as though he couldn't get enough of her. "You are so beautiful, you make my heart ache," he finally whispered.

"You know you don't have to say anything," she whispered back. "You've already won me over."

"I plan to keep winning you every day."

The phrase was similar to how her dad often described his efforts to show Mom love. The winning didn't just happen once on the wedding day. That was only the start of the winning that was intended to be an everyday occurrence.

"Then what are you waiting for?" She couldn't keep her voice from turning sultry. "Come here."

His lips curled up into a sexy half grin that made her stomach do a series of flips. He crossed to her, and as his fingers connected with hers, she tugged him down.

He dropped into the spot beside her and wrapped his arms around her as she pressed against him. Their mouths collided at the same time with an explosive need that had been growing all evening. His rhythm was powerful and hungry, and she loved it. She joined in the kiss just as powerfully and hungrily, eager to be kissing him again so passionately.

With his arms tightening, she could feel his wildly beating heart and guessed he could feel hers beating just as hard for him. This love between them was intense, probably because they were both intense people who felt things deeply. It would mean incredible highs, but would it also mean they might go through difficult lows?

She didn't want to think about that tonight, not on their wedding night.

It. Was. Her. Wedding. Night. How had she gotten to this point, and what was she going to do about it?

Her kissing came to a halt.

He immediately tamed his passion and broke the kiss. He rested his cheek against hers, his scruffy jaw grazing her and his heavy breathing filling her senses.

Was she scared? What was going on?

"Are you all right?" he whispered.

She nodded. She was all right. She really was. But... she wasn't sure that she was ready to do more than just kiss. All that really mattered was being close to him, even if that meant just curling up beside him. They would have their whole lives for everything else, which meant they didn't have to rush and could wait to be more intimate until they were alone.

"I think we need just a little more time before..." She struggled to find her next words. "Before we, well, you know."

"Yes, I know." He smoothed a hand over her hair. "I should like the first time I make love to my wife to be special and beautiful and meaningful, not something rushed and hushed."

She breathed out the tension that had started to build, and she let herself relax against him. "I love you even more for that."

He reclined onto the couch and pulled her down into the spot in front of him, the same way they'd slept the previous night. After he situated the blanket over them, he wrapped his arms around her and pressed a kiss to her head.

She snuggled back into him. "Max?"

"Yes, darling?"

"Just because we've agreed to wait on making love doesn't mean I want to wait on kissing you."

"Do not worry, my love. I do not want to wait on that either." His fingers combed back strands of her hair, and in the next instant, his lips were upon her neck, hot and hard and heavy.

She gasped her pleasure and arched into him. If this was what she had to look forward to tonight, she would not complain in the least.

20

Three full days trapped in the mountains, and now they were well into their fourth.

Max had expected to be able to leave by now. At the very least, he had anticipated that a rescue operation would have arrived. But they had not seen a single living creature since arriving, not even a bird.

Emberly had speculated that the wind conditions had prevented an air rescue and that the arctic temperatures and heavy snow accumulations had halted anyone from reaching them by land.

With her fishing line down the crude hole they had sawn in the ice, Emberly peered up at the sky—the first blue, sunny sky they'd had since the start of their journey. "Kade could at least drop off more supplies for us, even if he can't land his chopper."

After rationing what little food they'd had, they had eaten the last morsels the previous evening. Now, today, their hunger was keen.

The snow was too deep for the snowshoes. But with the clearer weather, Emberly had hoped they might be able to ride out on the snowmobiles. Unfortunately, the batteries on both would not start due to the below-freezing temperature.

They had also turned on one of the phones and attempted to make contact again. But still they had not been able to connect to any service, not even for a simple text.

After their failed attempts at rescuing themselves, Emberly had suggested they do a little ice fishing. Max hadn't objected, especially because his stomach was protesting its lack of sustenance. Thankfully, the cabin had a pair of fishing poles, extra fishing line, as well as a small tackle box with artificial bait.

Dressed in as many layers as they had, he and Emberly had used the snowshoes and managed to hike to the lake through the trail they had shoveled. The ice had been difficult to break through, but Emberly knew a few tricks, and eventually they had created a hole big enough to allow them to fish.

He jiggled his line again, hoping the fish below would not notice that the colorful minnow was fake.

They had been outside the cabin for less than an hour, and already his fingers and toes stung from the cold. They would not be able to stay much longer before having to go back inside and thaw out. He just prayed they would catch fish first.

The rod in his hand bobbed, and he gripped it tighter with both gloved hands. "I do think I have a nibble."

Emberly's attention shifted to his pole just as it bent and the line turned taut. Her cheeks and nose were red from the cold, and her eyes filled with sudden excitement. "Hurry, jerk upward."

He did as she'd shown him that day on the ranch when they'd gone ice fishing. He tugged the rod and could feel the fish digging into the hook, wiggling and trying to break free.

He held on tightly, hunger driving him to be careful and yet strong in his quest to catch the fish. If they were stuck at the cabin for another day, he not only wanted the sustenance for himself but for Emberly and Braun and Winzig. But mostly Emberly.

As he strained to lift the rod, a fish glistened on the end of the line.

"A brook trout." Emberly grabbed onto his rod too. "And it's at least sixteen inches!" Her smile was brilliant and beautiful.

For a second, he wanted to stop time and stand there and admire her.

As dire as their situation was becoming, she had maintained good spirits and did not become easily discouraged. She always enjoyed whatever they were doing, whether playing cards, shoveling paths, looking for kindling, or simply sipping coffee. Now, though cold and hungry, she was having fun ice fishing.

Although he was naturally more of a worrier, he was learning from her to take one day at a time, to find the little things to be thankful for, and even to appreciate being at the cabin, where they could focus much on each other without the distractions of real life.

Surprisingly, the days had gone quickly, and the nights had flown by as well. He would not deny that he loved the nights best of all, when he had the chance to be alone with her. They lay on the couch together, kissing and talking and kissing some more. They slept off and on, waking to kiss again. He could never get enough of her, and he was glad that she seemed to feel the same way.

He bent down, touched her lips with his, and stole a quick kiss.

Her smile only widened, and the sunlight turned her eyes amber. She reached up and kissed him back.

Then she began to take the hook out of the fish's jaw. "This will easily feed all four of us."

It was big, but he did not have the heart to tell her he could eat the whole thing himself and still have room for more.

As she dropped his line with the hook and bait still intact, she nodded at her pole, which she'd propped up in a drift. "I want to see if I'm able to catch something too, but I have to be honest. I can hardly feel my toes and fingers and should probably head back."

He frowned as he began to gather their supplies. "Why did you not tell me you were so cold, darling?"

"I'm fine, Max." She set the fish aside and began to strap on one of her snowshoes. "Numb fingers and toes are worth it now that we have something to eat."

She'd hardly spoken the words when she froze and spun to face the western edge of the lake.

"What is it?" He scanned the thick woodland, the pine boughs bent under the weight of heavy blankets of snow.

"I hear a chopper."

Max paused his breathing and strained to listen. In the silence of the high mountain lake, he caught the faint sound of a motor and blades. Relief swelled inside and made him suddenly weak. Help was finally on the way.

She finished strapping on her other snowshoe. "We need to try to flag Kade down. I think he could land on the lake and the ice would hold him."

Max hurriedly donned his snowshoes and joined her away from the trees and out in the open, where hopefully Kade would be able to see them.

As the helicopter grew louder and then came into sight, Emberly started to wave her arms. "Kade! Here!"

Max joined her in flailing his arms and shouting, although he doubted anyone could hear them above the noise of the helicopter.

The helicopter was too far away during its first pass and did not notice them. As it circled back, he and Emberly began waving again, and this time the helicopter flew closer. It was clear the moment someone spotted them, because the pilot swerved around and made a direct line toward them. As it hovered lower, they could see two figures through the front window: Kade and Tyler.

Emberly was hiking and motioning toward the shore, probably an area that had thicker ice than out where they'd been fishing. Max followed after her. A moment later, Kade seemed to catch on to her silent instructions and directed the helicopter to a smooth stretch of the frozen and snow-covered lake.

Since the snow was so powdery, the power of the blades caused the snow to swirl and fly in every direction, blinding Max and Emberly and forcing them to stop. Thankfully, within minutes, Kade had landed the helicopter in the clearing. As soon as the blades stopped whirring, Emberly was once again racing toward the helicopter as fast as her snowshoes would allow her.

Tyler jumped out first and tried to move through the snow toward them. But he sank nearly thigh-deep in the snow and could hardly move. Kade climbed out next and tried to wade toward them but was unsuccessful too.

Emberly reached them first and fell into Tyler's arms.

He hugged her tight. "You all right?"

"We're just fine." She pulled back and was swept up into a hug by Kade.

Both of the men were bundled in heavy winter gear and boots, clearly prepared for the harsh conditions.

Tyler met Max's gaze and nodded what appeared to be a friendly greeting. At the very least, he was not scowling at Max as he usually did.

Max nodded back. His nerves were already tightening in defense, knowing he would have a battle ahead when he revealed that he and Emberly had gotten married. Tyler would likely be displeased, to put it mildly.

Kade drew Emberly into the crook of his arm and squeezed her. "We're sorry we couldn't make it up here sooner. But the wind didn't let up until the middle of last night. We wanted to start out right away, but Dad told us to wait until daylight."

"Don't worry." Emberly leaned into her brother. "I figured you'd come when you could."

"The others?" Tyler asked, his eyes still filled with worry.

"They are at the cabin," Max replied.

Emberly glanced back toward the center of the lake. "Max and I came out to fish since we ran out of food last night."

"So you just ran out?" Kade was examining them both as though making sure they were okay. "Dad thought the place was stocked enough to get you through a few days."

"We had to ration the supplies to get us to today, and we're hungry. We caught one fish, a sixteen-inch brook trout. But we were too cold to stay out and catch more."

Tyler turned back to the helicopter. "Come on. We've got hand and toe warmers."

After unstrapping their snowshoes, Emberly and Max were hoisted into the helicopter and told to warm up, then Tyler and Kade strapped on their own snowshoes and set out to the cabin to retrieve Braun and Winzig.

While they were gone, Max did his best to help Emberly warm her fingers and toes. Once she was well on her way to thawing, they began eating the nuts and energy bars Kade and Tyler had brought along.

"Are you getting warm now, darling?" Max had drawn Emberly against him on the seat, hoping to lend her his body heat.

"I'm doing better." She had only eaten half of her bar and handed the remainder to him. "Here. I'm done."

"Thank you, my love. But I want you to eat it. I shall be fine until we reach the ranch." He had already eaten two bars and two packages of nuts, making sure to leave enough for both Winzig and Braun. The food had taken away the harshness of his hunger, but obviously Emberly sensed he was still famished.

She broke off a piece and held it up to his mouth.

He pressed his lips together.

She smiled at him innocently. "When should we tell

my brothers about our marriage?"

"Whenever you would—"

She cut him off by shoving the piece of energy bar into his mouth.

He had no choice but to chew and swallow. "I see what you are—"

She stuffed the remainder of the bar in his mouth, her smile turning decidedly smug and making him want to kiss that smugness away until she was breathless.

He loved this woman more than life. That was what the past few days had shown him. The time together had also shown him that he wanted to spend his life devoted to making sure she knew how much he loved her.

As he finished eating the bar, he shifted and took off her hat. He tossed it to the floor and then reached for the tip of her braid. Locking eyes with hers, he tugged loose the hair tie and began to unravel her hair.

Over the past couple of days and nights, he had loved the freedom he now had to touch her and kiss her, including combing his fingers through her hair. Her hair was thick and silky and glorious, and he reveled in undoing it and undoing her in the process, because she always took great pleasure in having his hands in her hair.

It had grown increasingly harder with each passing night to hold himself back, especially because the desire between them was only getting stronger. However, he had honored his word to her that they would wait.

Regardless, he was not above taunting her just a little. As he unwound her braid, he bent in and brushed a kiss on her jaw, then one below her ear.

Her lashes fluttered down, and she tilted her head to afford him more of her graceful neck to kiss.

He pulled back, caressing her hair but nothing more.

She tried to tug him closer. "Max." Her voice was breathless with need.

Another bolt of heat shot through him, but he didn't budge, even though he wanted to keep kissing her. Instead, he gave her a wicked smile in return.

She pushed at him and laughed lightly. Then before he could tease her again, she wrapped her arms around his neck and shifted so that she was sitting on his lap.

"You should know something," she whispered as she brushed her lips across his.

He almost groaned out his desire but managed to somehow speak coherently. "And what is that, darling?"

"You will never win. I will always find a way to drive you crazier than you do me." She finished her statement by jerking his shirt out of his jeans and sliding her hand underneath and over the bare skin of his abdomen. At the same time, she teased him again with another ghost of a kiss.

He was suddenly on fire. And he knew she was right. She would drive him to the brink of insanity. But he loved it and would not have it any other way, although he would not tell her so.

Instead, he wound his fingers deeper into her hair and guided her mouth to his, fusing them together powerfully and magnetically. When they came together like that, he felt as though their destinies had been intertwined. He'd been a lost comet circling endlessly until she'd come along like a shooting star. They'd collided and now were both burning brightly together.

Her passion, her enthusiasm, and her momentum with each kiss always seeped through him and brought him an energy and life that he'd never known. A part of him was beginning to wonder how he'd ever lived without her. He knew without a doubt that he needed her and that he would be hopelessly lost if something ever pulled them apart.

As their mouths danced to the passionate rhythm of their kiss, he fisted her hair tighter. She made a soft, pleasurable noise in her throat and then dug her fingers into his hair. Her grip tightened, and she pressed her body to his.

This universe with just the two of them enveloped in their passion was the only place he wanted to live. Yet this passion was only a foretaste of what was still possible between them.

Soon.

Very soon.

He deepened the fusing of their mouths and earned

another throaty groan from her. He was so lost in their kiss that he barely heard the helicopter door opening, barely heard the growl behind him, and hardly felt the hand gripping his shirt until he was being yanked backward.

"I knew this would happen!" Tyler's shout reverberated through the helicopter. "That you would help yourself and take advantage of Emberly."

"Tyler!" Emberly shouted as she slipped off Max's lap and onto the floor.

Tyler had pulled Max's shirt up to his throat so that it was strangling him. At the same time, he was dragging him through the helicopter door as though he intended to toss him out and leave him in the cold wilderness alone.

"You are a lying piece of scum!" Tyler roared.

From the corner of his eye, Max could see Kade hurrying toward the helicopter with Braun and Winzig traipsing along more slowly, still on the path that led to the cabin.

"Let go of Max!" Emberly scrambled up from the floor and lunged after her brother. "Right now!"

Max clawed for purchase of something and managed to grab the helicopter door.

Tyler jerked at him, attempting to dislodge his hold. "He thinks he can have anything he wants, but he can't have you."

Emberly seized Max's arm and tried hauling him

back, her forehead furrowed with a scowl. "Max has every right to kiss me!"

"It's obvious he wants a whole lot more than kissing!" Tyler shouted in return. "That's probably why he brought you up here, so that he could pressure you into more."

"Absolutely not," Max interjected, even though Tyler was still cutting off his breathing with his shirt pulled too tight.

Tyler heaved again, but Max held fast.

"Stop!" Emberly screamed. "Max is my husband!"

The words rang out in the silence of the frigid winter wonderland. Only steps away from the helicopter, Kade froze.

Tyler grew motionless as well.

Emberly used the moment to latch onto Max. Thankfully, Tyler loosened his grip at the same time that Max tugged himself loose and stumbled backward toward her. She reached for him, as if somehow that would rescue him from her brother's wrath.

But Max doubted anything would save him from Tyler murdering him, not even Winzig, who was navigating through the snow as fast as he could, his expression lethal.

Emberly pressed at Max, pushing him onto the seat they'd just vacated. Max wanted to resist, wanted to defend himself, but he literally could not stand in the helicopter. Besides, rather than have another physical altercation with Tyler, Max knew he needed to seek a peaceful resolution.

Emberly plopped back down on his lap, giving them no other choice but to work out the situation more graciously. She lifted her chin and glared at Tyler. "Max and I got married here at the cabin."

Tyler stared silently for another moment before narrowing his eyes. "Common law marriage might still be legal in Colorado, but it won't work in our family."

She shook her head. "It's not common law—"

"And self-solemnization without an officiant is not okay in our family either."

"That's not what we did."

Max was not familiar with Colorado laws regarding marriage, but apparently a couple could get legally married without a ceremony or officiants. If so, then their marriage would be acceptable in the state as well as his country.

Before Emberly could say more, Max spoke up. "We were married by my personal assistant, Braun, who is a licensed registrar in Karltenberg. He performed the ceremony, and it was witnessed by my protection agent."

At that moment, Winzig finally made it to Tyler, wrapped an arm around his neck, and put him in a headlock. Kade started to climb onto Winzig's back, but the protection agent swung around in a fluid move and flipped Kade over, never once relinquishing his tight grip on Tyler.

For a moment no one moved, probably too surprised by Winzig's power.

Kade lay sprawled out in the snow, staring straight up at the sky. He finally cracked a smile. "That was some move."

Max expelled a breath. "I do apologize. I should have warned you not to touch me or Winzig."

Kade sat up. "Should have known that, as a prince, you'd have a really good protection agent."

A prince?

It was Max's turn to freeze. How did Kade know he was a prince?

Tyler was watching him now too, with knowing eyes. Did they all realize he was a prince? If so, how had they discovered it?

Max nodded at Winzig, giving him permission to release Tyler.

Winzig let go of Tyler and pushed him away from the helicopter door.

Tyler straightened and stretched his neck. "When you didn't return to your country on schedule, your father got worried and contacted us."

"Of course." Max had been so enamored with Emberly that he hadn't taken into account that his father and family would be wondering what had become of him.

"Your disappearance has become international news," Kade added, standing and brushing the snow from his snowsuit.

Max should have realized the tumult his disappearance would cause.

Even though he would have preferred to be the one to confess his royalty to Emberly's family, at least now they knew. He could only pray they would accept that he loved Emberly and intended to be the best husband to her that any man could be.

21

Emberly—still on Max's lap—reached for his hand as the helicopter began its descent. Tyler's attack had brought them both back to the reality that their marriage would be controversial and they would likely have more conflict ahead—hopefully no more physical altercations though.

Max squeezed her hand even though he'd been distracted for the short duration of their ride.

"The reporters have been swarming the ranch since the story broke two days ago," Kade said through his headset as he nodded in the direction of the ranch entrance. "Someone will have to inform them you guys have been rescued so they go away."

Emberly peered out the window at snow-covered foothills to the sight of vehicles, camera crews, and reporters swarming the area outside the locked gate. Security personnel stood nearby, making sure no one came past.

Her family had learned to keep out reporters and paparazzi during many of Brock's visits home. But they'd never had a prince to protect or a story of international importance.

Max glanced down at the people milling about, some of them now pointing at the helicopter with camera lenses that could probably see right inside.

He sat back out of sight and tugged Emberly back with him. "I shall go and speak with them directly."

"I can go with you."

His brow had a worried line in it that had only gotten deeper with every passing minute.

In the front seat next to Kade, Tyler hadn't spoken for much of the ride. From the way his jaw was clenching, she knew he was frustrated about her and Max getting married. But he'd probably refrained from saying or doing anything else because he didn't want to earn another headlock from Winzig, who was kneeling on the floor while Braun sat in the second passenger seat.

Emberly was disappointed that neither of her brothers had been more excited for her. But what had she expected? Their lack of support was partially why she'd decided to go through with marrying Max at the cabin.

As Kade directed the helicopter to the landing pad on a plateau above the family house, the back door of the house opened, and her mom and dad exited along with Kinsey and Wyatt, all in heavy coats and boots and hats.

No doubt they were all worried about her.

Tyler had already called them after they'd reached cell phone range and let everyone know they were all okay. Since all of their phones were dead, Tyler had asked Dad to alert Max's family that he'd been found and was doing fine.

Emberly shifted and caught Max's gaze. Even though he offered her a small smile and brushed his thumb across the back of her hand, the gravity in his eyes did nothing to ease the worry growing inside her. Did he regret their hasty marriage? Was he concerned about how to tell his family, the same way she was hesitant about how to tell hers?

She hoped he wasn't having regrets. The only regret she was beginning to have was that they'd had to leave their secluded bubble out in the wilderness, where they could be together and love each other without anyone condemning them. Even though they'd been stranded and hungry, at least they'd had a blissful time together.

As the helicopter touched the ground, Emberly silently rehearsed the words to explain to her parents all that had happened.

"I'd like to be the one to tell Mom and Dad about Max," she said to Kade and Tyler as she stepped down from the helicopter onto the landing.

Mom and Dad had just ascended the stairs and were already crossing toward her. She barely had time to take a few steps before they were gathering her into their arms tightly.

She hugged Kinsey and Wyatt and then embraced Mom and Dad again as Wyatt and Kinsey went to Tyler and hopefully distracted him from spilling the news about her marriage.

"I was trying not to worry too much," Dad said as he pulled back. "I knew you had all the skills necessary to survive out there."

"Even so." Mom cupped Emberly's cheek as she blinked back tears. "We didn't know if you'd decided to stay at the cabin or gotten caught in the snowstorm on the way down."

"I made the decision to stay since I didn't know if we could make it down before the conditions got worse."

"That was a wise choice, darlin'." Dad shifted toward Max, who was standing beside her. "I'm sorry for all the worry this has caused your family, Max."

"I apologize that you are having to deal with the media." Max stood tall and regal. "I also apologize that you had to learn about my true identity through this mishap."

Dad waved a hand. "Oh, don't worry. I already knew. The minute you started showing interest in Emberly, I had one of my connections do a private investigation to learn more about you."

"Da-ad. Was that really necessary?" No wonder her

brothers were so overprotective. They had inherited that trait from Dad.

He shrugged, his grin turning crooked. "I'm sorry. It probably wasn't necessary. But you are my only daughter, and I couldn't let you spend time with a man I didn't approve of."

"I was well aware of Max's royalty, and we were keeping it under wraps so that we didn't end up with the press at our gates." She gave him a pointed look.

Dad raised his gloved hands. "Don't blame me. I didn't tell a soul. This only happened after Max's family released a press statement about his disappearance."

Max nodded. "I do believe the best thing I can do for the peace of your ranch is to go and make a quick appearance and then send them on their way."

"First," Emberly said quickly, reaching for Max's hand, "Mom, Dad, there's something you should know."

Both of her parents stared at her hand intertwined with Max's. What would they think? Would her mom be upset that she hadn't been able to help her only daughter plan a big wedding? Would her dad be frustrated that Max hadn't asked permission to have her hand in marriage?

She swallowed hard and could feel Max watching her.

"T.W., Leah." Max squeezed Emberly's hand. "I love your daughter."

Dad's smile began to rise again.

"I not only asked her to be my wife during our trip," Max continued quickly, "but I also suggested that we become man and wife while we were at the cabin."

Dad's smile quickly fell away, and he stared with an open mouth at Max.

Emberly forced a smile. "We're married. Max is my husband."

Mom's eyes had widened, but otherwise, she didn't move.

Emberly held her breath. Tyler, Kinsey, and Wyatt had grown silent, clearly overhearing the conversation. Kade was closing up the helicopter, and he paused too, probably waiting for Mom and Dad's reaction.

"You're not joking?" Dad spluttered.

"They are not, sir." Braun stood a short distance away. "I performed the ceremony."

Dad's brown eyes came to rest on Emberly's face again, and he seemed to be looking for something there. "Do you love Max?" he asked quietly.

"Yes." She leaned her head against Max's arm. "I love Max more than anything."

Dad shifted and studied Max's face with the same intensity as before, holding out a hand to Max. "Welcome to the family, son."

"Thank you." Max shook her dad's hand.

Then Dad turned to her and drew her into another hug. "He's a good man, Emberly. Real good."

"He is." She breathed out her relief at her dad's easy acceptance of the situation.

As Dad released her, Mom grabbed her into a hug too. "Congratulations, honey."

Emberly clung to her mom. "You're not too disappointed that I didn't have a big wedding?"

Mom pulled back but held onto Emberly's arms. "Not at all. I'm getting to help Kinsey with hers, and I'll learn to be satisfied with that."

They chatted more about the simple cabin wedding as they made their way down from the landing pad to the house. Once there, Max asked Kade to take him to the gate so that he could talk to the reporters.

"Are you okay?" she asked as they stood by the back doorway while waiting for Kade.

Max took her hands in his. "I regret the strain my family must have experienced in not knowing about my welfare."

"I'm sure they would love hearing from you personally."

"Yes, I am sure they would."

She held out a hand toward Kade. "Let Max use your phone."

Within no time, Max was on the phone with his family. He walked a short distance away to have privacy, so she couldn't hear what he told them. He spoke for only a few moments before returning to her, the worry line in his forehead not as deep.

She wanted to kiss any remaining worry away. In fact, she wanted to kiss him regardless of any reason other than the fact that they hadn't kissed in a while and she was craving a kiss.

Instead, she took his hand and intertwined their fingers. "What did they say about us being married?"

"I did not tell them."

A sense of uneasiness prickled her. "Oh."

"'Twas not the right moment." He glanced toward where Kade was waiting in the SUV he'd backed out of the garage. Winzig was in the passenger seat already, and the back door was open and waiting for Max.

"So when is the right time?" She couldn't stop herself from pressuring Max. After all, she'd told her family almost the moment they'd arrived home so that it was out in the open and she didn't have to hide anything.

"I shall tell them soon, but not tonight." He bent and pressed a kiss to her forehead, then strode away.

She could only watch him with a growing sense that things were changing now that they were back to normal life. Was he pulling away from her already? Was the bond they'd formed at the cabin loosening?

Maybe it had formed because of the forced proximity or because of the strain of being stranded in a snowstorm. What if he already regretted their rash decision to get married?

She pushed aside her concerns and went inside with her family. Mom immediately began helping Anson prepare breakfast for her and Max, starting eggs and bacon cooking as well as heating the griddle for pancakes.

Emberly took a stool at the counter beside her dad and Wyatt, while Tyler and Kinsey hovered nearby.

They had turned on the monitor that showed the footage of the front gate so they could watch Max when he spoke to the press.

The family SUV came into view and halted near the gate. A few seconds later, Max exited from the back. The flash of cameras and the shouts of reporters filled the air.

Max approached the gate, waited for it to open while Winzig stood on one side of him and Kade on the other. When the gate was fully open, Max held up a hand, likely to ask for silence. After a moment, the reporters stopped calling out questions and grew quiet.

"Thank you," his voice came through the monitor. Though they could only see him from the back due to the angle of the security camera, it was enough to view his stiff shoulders and tall, proud bearing.

For a minute or two, Max explained how he'd gone out snowshoeing and gotten caught in the storm, but he'd been safe in a cabin for the past few days until the rescue this morning.

"All is well," he concluded. "Everyone in our party has returned, and other than being a little hungry and ragged, we are unharmed and glad to be back. Thank you for your concern and well-wishes."

He pivoted and started back to the SUV. But the reporters began to volley questions. "Is it true you were together with Emberly McQuaid?" "Is Emberly McQuaid your newest lover?" "Are you having a fling with Emberly McQuaid?"

From her spot at the counter, Emberly snorted at the brazen questions. "That's all they care about? Whether Max and I slept together?"

Beside her, Wyatt paused in eating a piece of toast and peered up at her with wide eyes. "Did you have a sleepover, Aunt Emberly?"

Before she could answer her nephew, Kade took a step toward the reporters, his face contorted with anger. "For your information," he called above the questions, "my sister and the prince are married, so why don't you just stop with all the speculations."

At the news, chaos seemed to break out among the reporters, this time causing a hailstorm of questions. "Prince Max, are you really married to Emberly McQuaid?" "When were you married?" "How long have you known Miss McQuaid?"

Max had halted, and his back was stiff.

Emberly stared at the monitor, hardly able to breathe. How would he respond to the questions?

He stood unmoving.

She could see his profile harden and his jaw tighten.

Then he turned around and returned to the spot at the gate. He faced the reporters directly, and they once again grew mostly silent. "Yes, I recently married Emberly McQuaid. She is my wife, and we plan to return to Karltenberg together."

Another barrage of questions rose into the air.

"We would like to keep our relationship private for now," Max called above the chaos. "Thank you for respecting our wishes."

"With the looming deadline of your thirty-fifth birthday, did you marry Miss McQuaid so hastily to avoid abdicating the throne to your brother?" The question in a heavy German accent came from a man at the front of the crowd.

To avoid abdicating the throne to his brother? What did that mean? Emberly's heart began to pound a strange rhythm.

Max shook his head curtly. "No, that was not the reason for our marriage."

"With the pressure from the king and parliament, you cannot deny that the marriage will solidify your position as the heir apparent."

What was this all about? Max had indicated pressure from his father to marry, but he'd never mentioned that he would have to abdicate if he didn't take a wife. Did he have to be married by his thirty-fifth birthday in order to keep his position as the heir apparent?

A sick weight dropped to the bottom of Emberly's stomach.

"My marriage to Emberly has nothing to do with that." Max's voice rose above the others that were calling out.

The same reporter with the same accent yelled out again. "But you cannot deny that you have been on the search for a wife in order to fulfill the king and parliament's deadline."

This time Max didn't respond, neither confirming nor denying the reporter. But it was clear enough to Emberly. There was a deadline, and it was fast approaching.

He nodded at Winzig as he moved aside. The burly man stepped into Max's place, braced his feet apart, and crossed his arms. Once again, Max headed toward the SUV with Kade following.

Emberly could only stare at the monitor, the sickness inside swirling faster.

That was why Max had been in such a hurry to marry her. That was why he'd suggested they not wait for family or have a real wedding. Because he'd known he was running out of time and needed to get the deal done before it was too late.

Her dad turned off the monitor, plunging the room into silence except for the sizzling of the bacon and eggs.

No one around her moved, except Wyatt, who was still eating his toast.

She hadn't misunderstood Max. No, her whole family had heard him admit to having to marry by his birthday or lose the opportunity to become the next king of his country.

She sat frozen to the stool, but her mind was racing with a thousand thoughts. Had Max come to the ranch on a mission to find a wife? Had he targeted her because she looked gullible and easy to win over? The woman who'd failed out of college, who couldn't do anything better than work on her family's ranch, who relied on her brothers to bail her out of trouble?

Why else would he want an unimportant, untitled woman like her when he could have any other woman?

Of course, he couldn't plan a snowstorm, but maybe he'd intended to find a way to force their proximity. That's probably why Braun had his license as a registrar, because then he could marry the naive American woman who fell for Max's charm.

Her dad reached for her hand. "I'm sure there's a good explanation, darlin'."

Instead of proving to her family she was strong and independent and adequate, she'd shown them all over again what a failure she was, this time in her marriage.

She pulled back from Dad and hopped off the stool. A tightness moved up into her lungs and then her throat.

Even if she could have managed a response, she didn't want to talk to anyone.

She made her way to the back door.

"Emberly, wait." Her mom's footsteps pattered after her.

Emberly was already at the back door by the time her mom caught her arm. "Honey, please. Let's wait for Max to return."

Tears stung Emberly's eyes, and she blinked them back. "No. I don't want to talk to Max." The words tumbled out broken and breathless. Then before anyone else could stop her, she raced off toward the trail that led down to her cottage.

All she wanted to do was get inside, lock the door, and cry in private.

22

Max leaned his head against Emberly's door. "Please, darling. Please. Let me see you."

Silence greeted him on the other side, just as it had for the past hours that he'd been outside her cottage, knocking and trying to talk to her.

He expelled a long, frustrated sigh—one directed at himself. He had made an utter mess of everything, and he had no idea how to repair the damage.

Right after the questions at the gate—the ones directed at his motivation for marrying Emberly—he'd had an uneasy feeling. As he'd walked away from the reporters, he'd silently berated himself for not being completely honest with Emberly about the looming deadline for his getting married. He should have told her about it when he'd first suggested marriage, and he should have reassured her that the deadline did not factor into his desire to marry her so quickly.

During the winding drive back up to the house, he had planned to pull her aside and tell her about the deadline and the pressure to abdicate. He had wanted to let her know before she saw something online or was confronted by a reporter herself.

As he'd stepped out of the SUV, he had been met by an angry Tyler, who had almost punched him. With Winzig there, Tyler had resorted to a tirade about being a lying, conniving piece of horse manure for using Emberly and hurting her.

Max hadn't needed anyone to tell him that she'd heard the exchange with the reporter and knew about his need to marry or lose the throne. When he'd brushed past Tyler and gone into the house, Leah had informed him that Emberly wasn't there and had rushed off to her cottage.

He'd gone after Emberly, and he hadn't left her stoop since, not even when Braun had pleaded with him on several occasions that he needed to eat and shower and take care of himself.

Max was cold and hungry and tired, but he had not been able to make himself leave her door. He was not sure he could ever make himself go. A part of him was determined to live on her front porch until she finally came out and had to face him and listen to him explain that their rushed wedding had nothing to do with his becoming king.

However, as he'd waited outside her door the past hours, he had asked himself over and over if ulterior motives had played a role in pressuring her to marry him at the cabin. He still was not entirely sure if his subconscious had prompted him to a degree. But he was one hundred percent certain he had fallen in love with her and that he wanted to be married to her regardless of whether or not he ever became king.

He had told her that and a great deal of other thoughts throughout the past hours. He hadn't known if she was listening, but he had confessed to everything, had begged her to forgive him for not telling her sooner, had explained how it had not been his intent to withhold information from her.

But no amount of talking had swayed her to open the door, and neither had any of his long, rambling texts. She had shut him out thoroughly and completely—not just out of the cottage but out of her life.

He couldn't blame her. The situation did appear devious on his part, as if he really had coerced her into marriage. If the roles were reversed, he might be hurt and confused as well. He needed her to know his love for her was real and that it wasn't a means to an end. That was why he was still standing on her stoop, waiting, hoping, and needing to see her.

He pressed the door with one hand, wishing he had the strength to break it down and force his way inside.

But he knew he couldn't force Emberly, not even if he was that strong. He wanted her willingly or not at all.

"I promise I did not marry you so that I could keep the crown." He listened for any sign of her—breathing, shuffling, anything—but he could hear nothing. As far as he knew, she might be in her bed, covers piled over her head and the bedroom door closed.

A manly hand clamped his shoulder, companionably and kindly.

Max began to shrug it off. "Not yet, Braun."

"It's me, son." At the sound of T.W.'s voice, Max hung his head even lower.

"I apologize, T.W., for causing this disaster." Max had caught glimpses of Tyler and Kade lurking around the cottage from time to time through the morning and early afternoon. They had come to check on Emberly too. Or perhaps they had been keeping an eye on him to make sure he behaved.

T.W. did not immediately respond, but neither did he remove his grasp from Max's shoulder.

Max shifted to find T.W. in a heavy winter coat, peering at him with shadowed eyes. Leah stood a short distance away, also in her winter gear. Beyond them stood Tyler and Kinsey. Max didn't need T.W. to speak to know what this meeting was about. They wanted him to leave the ranch.

"You're a good man, Max." T.W. squeezed his

shoulder before letting go. "I'm glad to have you as part of the family."

"You are? Even after all that has occurred? After all the trouble I am bringing upon your family?"

"Of course I'm glad." T.W.'s expression was graver than usual. "I know you love Emberly. You've proven it again by standing out here for hours and not giving up on her."

The cold swirled around Max, and he was numb despite the hand and feet warmers Braun had been bringing him. Even so, he wasn't ready to go. "I would stand here the rest of the day and night—"

"But you should give her some time."

Max shook his head, frustration welling up within him. "I want to clarify that the birthday deadline did not enter my mind during my pursuit of your daughter. The truth is that I am utterly and completely enamored of her and wanted to marry her because I cannot imagine life without her in it."

T.W.'s expression softened, and he offered Max a small smile. "I believe you."

Max's chest squeezed with emotion. "Thank you."

T.W. nodded. "I have confidence you can work this out with her. But give yourself and her a break, why don't you?"

From T.W.'s tone, Max gathered the words were less of a suggestion and more of a command. Though Max did not want to walk away without some assurance that Emberly was okay, he had to give her a break. Maybe during the interim, she would read some of his texts and his apologies and affirmations of how much he loved her.

"Listen, son." T.W. dropped his voice. "You decided she's your one and only. Now you've got to make sure she knows she's your world, your everything, your life."

Frustration burned through Max. "How can I"—he kept his voice low too—"if she will not talk to me?"

"Most of the time, words just aren't enough."

Max tried to make sense of T.W.'s wise statement. "So you are saying talking may not work?"

"Talking is good and all. But you know the old saying: Actions speak louder than words."

"True enough."

T.W. gave his arm a squeeze, then backed down the step to the pathway. "You'll figure something out."

But what? What could he possibly do to prove to Emberly he intended to love her the way T.W. had previously encouraged him to—so completely that he would die for her?

As T.W. shuffled toward his wife, Max's mind began to spin with a plan, a way to show Emberly she was not only his one and only but his world, his everything, his life. Maybe he wouldn't actually die for her in this situation, but he could show her he was willing to sacrifice everything to have her.

23

At the banging against the front door of the cottage, Emberly pulled the covers over her head and burrowed deeper into her pillows.

After a restless night, she wasn't sure how long she'd been sleeping, but her body still felt sluggish, her eyelids were heavy, and her head ached. She had no desire to get out of bed and wanted to make it her permanent place of residence.

"Emberly, answer the door." Kade's voice outside her cottage was followed by more pounding.

She peeked past her comforter to find daylight streaming through her bedroom window over the simple furnishings and her simple bed. It was a new morning. That meant the worst day of her life was finally over—the day she'd discovered the man she was totally and madly in love with had married her because he needed a wife by his thirty-fifth birthday in order to become the next king of his country.

Apparently, kings weren't single and had to have wives. Who knew?

She should have known. After all, every king in history had wanted a wife to bear him children—particularly sons who could inherit the kingdom. Why would Max be any different?

In googling the laws of Karltenberg last night under her covers and in between fits of crying, she'd learned there wasn't a law requiring the heir apparent to get married. But the son in line to be king had always taken a wife, usually by the time he was in his mid-twenties. Max being in his thirties and still unmarried had created some unrest.

She also hadn't needed to search the internet much further to discover the king and parliament's pressure upon Max to choose a wife by his thirty-fifth birthday. How had she missed the articles during her previous searches? She supposed she'd been more focused on his personal and family history and hadn't been paying attention to articles that mentioned the king and parliament.

This time, though, she was keenly interested in discovering anything she could on an ultimatum by the king and parliament. The news articles made it seem as if Max had very little choice in the matter, that he would either need to marry or allow someone more settled—like his brother Alex—to take his place.

He'd already proven what a top-notch leader he was as the CEO of KWB Group. Every article praised him for his skills and abilities in making the bank so successful and expanding it throughout the world.

If he could lead the bank so well, he would be an excellent ruler of his country.

Actually, there was no doubt in Emberly's mind that Max would be a good king. During his visit at the ranch and while he'd been stranded with her at the cabin, she'd seen easily enough how much Max loved Karltenberg. He had been ready, willing, and eager to be king.

She also had no doubt that Max was ready, willing, and eager to have a wife so that he could move into his role as king with the approval of his father and his people.

That's why he'd been considering marrying Sarah—because an arranged marriage would appease his father and parliament. So why not marry an innocent and willing American who he found more attractive than Sarah? Especially a woman who would fall for him in no time at all.

Emberly blew out a raspberry. She'd fallen all right. And part of her hadn't even seen herself tripping and tumbling. It had happened so fast.

"Emberly, if you don't open up," Kade's voice echoed through the house, "you'll force me to get the master key and come in."

So, so fast. Fast, furious, and forever. Yes, she'd experienced the McQuaid legacy of love and had realized it wasn't just for the men in the family after all, that she could have it too...

Except that her husband had married her for what she could do for him and not because he loved her in return, hadn't he?

His twenty-plus texts said otherwise, as did the dozen or more voicemails.

He'd also stood outside her cottage door for hours—at least four—before her dad had convinced him to leave. She knew because she'd been sitting on the floor against the door for most of that time, listening to Max try to convince her that their marriage and his love for her were genuine. He'd claimed many times that the birthday deadline had not crossed his mind when he'd decided he wanted to marry her.

Logically, she knew he couldn't fake the affection she'd felt from him. He wouldn't have kissed her the way he had if there hadn't been at least some depth of feelings.

Even so, she hadn't been able to convince herself he was telling the truth as her heart had been breaking and the tears had streaked her cheeks. When he'd left, he'd bumped the door, presumably with his head, and told her he loved her and that he would be back.

Then silence had descended.

"Emberly, I'm coming in!" came Kade's obnoxious call.

Her family had given her some space yesterday and last night. But now they were obviously done allowing her to wallow and had sent Kade.

Would he have Max with him?

Emberly scrambled out of bed and slipped into a sweatshirt to cover her pj's. Then she peeked into the mirror attached to her dresser to find that her hair was unruly and messy. Worse than that, her face looked splotchy and swollen.

At the rattle of a key in the lock, she grabbed a pair of thick socks from the pile of clean laundry on her dresser. She only managed to get one on before her front door burst open and heavy footsteps crossed her living area.

"Emberly." Kade's voice held concern.

"I'm not dead, Kade."

He appeared in the bedroom doorway, his face taut with worry. "Why didn't you answer? We were getting worried."

"I was sleeping." She pulled on the second sock and chanced a glance beyond Kade to the other room. No one else was there.

Her heart gave a thud of disappointment that echoed in the emptiness inside her. Even if Max had said he'd be back, why would he be here? She'd all but cut him out of her life.

"How are you doing this morning?" Kade's voice softened as he took her in.

"How do I look like I'm doing?" She couldn't keep the irritation from her voice.

"Like you miss Max and want to be with him."

She'd expected a snarky response from Kade, and at the gentleness in his voice, her throat closed up. She'd been away from Max for less than twenty-four hours, and already she missed him so keenly she was ready to put aside her hurt and hesitancies and listen to him. He deserved a chance to explain himself.

Had he made a mistake by withholding important information from her? Yes. But was the information really so terrible? So he'd been tasked by his father and parliament to get married by his thirty-fifth birthday. If that was a tiny part of his motivation for marrying her, it still didn't take away the fact that he loved her, did it?

At the opening and closing of her cottage door, her pulse leaped with fresh anticipation. Was that Max?

Once again, she peered past Kade, only to find Tyler standing on the rug inside the front door, regarding her somberly. Were her brothers there to convince her she'd made a mistake in marrying Max? That she should file for divorce or perhaps get an annulment?

She couldn't let them step in this time. She had to figure her future out for herself. And like it or not, she owed herself and Max at least one more honest conversation about what had really happened between them and how they really felt toward each other. She had to do that, regardless of how much her brothers might disapprove or try to hinder her.

Even though a part of her wanted to admit defeat and let her shoulders slump, she pushed them higher. "I know you both think I'm a screwup. But I need to figure out my problems with Max without your interfering."

"A screwup?" Kade's brow shot up. "What in the world, Emberly? Of course we don't think that."

"Everyone thinks that."

Tyler's expression grew stormy, and he began crossing the room. "What are you talking about?"

"I didn't finish college. I had to come back here because I had no other options. And everyone knows you and Dad gave me my job and that I didn't earn it."

Tyler pushed past Kade and stepped into her bedroom. With both of her big, brawny brothers in the room, it seemed to shrink. Although she wanted to avoid the discussion and force them both to leave, she supposed it was past time to get the issue out in the open.

Tyler crossed his arms and glared at her. "You are incredibly smart. And you're talented at what you do. That's why we gave you the job."

"I got the job because Karen turned it down."

"Do you really think we would have offered you a job as event manager at the country's premier luxury ranch if we didn't think you were qualified?"

"I don't have a degree—"

Tyler scoffed. "The position is way too important to give to someone out of pity. We chose you because we knew you were the best person for the job, even better than Karen. We offered it to her first because of her seniority."

Emberly's heart gave a strange leap. Was that true?

"The fact is, you're one of the smartest and savviest people I know, and I really admire you." Tyler's tone gentled. "I'm just sorry I've never said it before now."

"I agree with Ty one hundred percent," Kade said.

"Besides, having a college degree doesn't define a person," Tyler continued. "There's a lot to be said for talent, intuition, and putting your all into learning and knowing a job—which is what you've got going for you."

She studied each of her brothers, their faces etched with sincerity. Maybe her insecurities were of her own making. She'd focused so much on what she thought was lacking in her life instead of looking at her strengths.

Was that true of her relationship with Max too? Was she subconsciously rejecting him and pushing him away because she didn't feel qualified to be his wife and a queen? Maybe she had to stop focusing on all the ways she would fall short of being what he needed and instead focus on all that she could do.

The need to see Max swelled sharply inside her. She wasn't sure if she could work things out with him. But she had to at least try and couldn't let her insecurities hold her back.

"Thanks, guys." She waved a hand to shoo her brothers from her room while crossing toward her closet. "Now you can go tell Mom and Dad I'm fine, that I'm done having a pity party for myself, and that I'm planning to track Max down and talk with him."

Neither of them budged and instead exchanged glances.

She halted in front of her closet door. "What?"

Kade met her gaze with a seriousness that she rarely saw in his eyes. "That's why we're here."

Her backbone stiffened with protest. "I let you interfere with Ryan, and I'm not doing that again."

Tyler held up his hands as though in surrender. "We're not trying to interfere—"

"Then stay out of things between me and Max."

"I know we need to get better at that," Kade interjected. "And we'll try. But—"

"No buts. I can handle this all on my own." She swung open the closet and began to browse through her outfit choices. "I'm assuming he's still staying at the house?"

Neither of her brothers answered.

As the silence lengthened, her neck prickled with uneasiness. She spun around and braced her hands on her hips. "What's wrong?"

Tyler met her gaze head-on. "Max left yesterday."

"Left?"

"Yep. He caught a plane back to Karltenberg last night."

She pinched the bridge of her nose. He'd left the ranch? The country? Her?

She shouldn't be surprised, not after shutting him out yesterday. Even so, she hadn't expected him to go without letting her know he was leaving. Maybe he was angry with her, had decided he didn't need her after all. Maybe he'd realized how crazy they'd been to get married so quickly.

Kade's lips tipped up into a smirk. "Don't worry. He still loves you."

"Then why did he leave?" Her voice cracked as the angst from the past day rushed out and attacked her like an army assailing an enemy.

"He met with us all last night before heading out," Tyler said, "and he let us know he's planning to meet with his father and the other leaders of his country to officially abdicate his right to the throne."

"What?" Her pulse began to speed, but it wasn't from relief. "He can't do that."

A crease formed in Kade's forehead. "He told us he wants to prove to you that he didn't marry you to gain the throne, that he married you for love alone. I thought you'd be happy about it."

"No, I'm not happy about it at all." She stood unmoving, even as her mind raced a thousand miles per hour. Yes, Max was noble in his desire to prove he loved her enough to give up the throne. And yes, he was noble to make such an enormous sacrifice for her. But . . . she couldn't let him give up being king. Not when it meant so much to him, and not when he would make such a great leader of his country.

She had to figure out what to do. But what?

She stared at her brothers, then stared at her open closet, then stared at her brothers again.

The turmoil churned faster. Time was slipping away. If he'd left last night, he was probably home by now, or very close to it. Would he go to see his father and parliament today?

No, she couldn't let him. Maybe she should call him and tell him he was making a big mistake. But what if he didn't answer her call? What if he wouldn't listen to her?

There really was only one thing to do to keep him from abdicating. And she would need everyone's help if she had any hope of accomplishing her mission.

24

Max's stomach was tied in a dozen knots as he paced the length of the Gold Drawing Room.

In the past forty-eight hours since leaving Emberly's cottage, he'd thought through every angle of his situation, and he had come to the same conclusion that he had at the ranch—he needed to abdicate his right to the throne.

Of course, he had hoped to tell his father as well as parliament yesterday. His overnight flight had landed in the early-morning hours in Zurich, the closest international airport to Vollenstadt. He had been exhausted and had not paid attention to where they were going until too late. Instead of going to the palace in Vollenstadt, their driver had taken him to the family estate on the Bodensee.

Rather than driving several more hours to reach the capital city, Braun had insisted they take the day to rest, refresh, and prepare for the meetings with his father and parliament. Although Max had not wanted to delay, Braun had complained of a headache and the need to sleep.

Reluctantly, Max had agreed to put off the encounters. Once he had, he'd realized the benefit of taking his time and not rushing the matter. His abdication of the throne was too important to do when he was hungry, disheveled, and sleep-deprived.

Today Max was feeling much more energetic. He'd also had time to rehearse what he intended to say, first to his father and then later to parliament. Unfortunately, parliament had a winter break and would not be convening until the following week.

In the meantime, however, he could speak to his father about the matter, arrange a meeting with Alex, and begin the process of handing over his succession to the throne.

Max paused beneath the center chandelier. Glittering with crystals that reflected the light, the ancient fixture was at least two meters across and hung low from the high ceiling, which was decorated with multiple roundels, each radiating gold lines. A frieze with rectangular panels ran around the tops of the walls, with delicate moldings of flowers, trees, and birds in each one.

One wall was filled with long windows decorated with golden curtains. The gold damask on a pair of settees shone with brilliance under the bright glow of the gold candelabras set on pedestal tables on either side of the enormous marble fireplace. An ornate piano that was painted gold graced the opposite side of the room and was surrounded by chairs upholstered in more gold damask.

Although the style and the lavishness of the gold were not to his liking, every item in the room—every vase, every rug, every mirror—had historical value and had been a part of the palace for decades, in some cases even centuries. Every item contained his heritage, and he was just as dedicated as Alex to preserving the ancient relics and buildings.

What would Alex say when he learned of the abdication?

His younger brother would dutifully step into the role without complaining. However, he would not relish it the same way he did his role as the curator and preserver of their family's many homes and treasures.

Max checked his watch again. It was well past eleven o'clock, the time Braun had arranged for him to meet with his father in the drawing room. His father was usually so punctual. What could be causing the delay?

Drawing in a breath to steady his nerves, Max started pacing again, lengthening his stride. As he reached a large, mirrored cabinet on one wall, the chamber door behind him opened, and Max stopped.

He pivoted to find a woman entering the drawing room on his father's arm. She was attired in heels, a classy slender skirt, and a blazer over a lacy top. At the sight of the red hair styled in an elegant chignon revealing beautiful facial features, so delicate and yet so strong, Max's heartbeat slammed against his chest.

Emberly?

She was speaking animatedly to Father in a friendly way. His father, who was an older version of Max with his tall bearing and blond hair, was smiling at Emberly and laughed lightly at something she said.

At the sight of him in front of the cabinet, the two came to a halt.

Emberly's warm brown eyes fixed on him and seemed to take him in as hungrily as he was taking her in.

The knots in his stomach began to loosen. Was she happy to see him?

As if hearing his unspoken question, her lips curved into a smile—one that contained tenderness. Her eyes lit up too, and he was suddenly breathless with the need to be with her and talk to her and find out how she was doing.

It had nearly killed him to walk away from her cottage two days ago and leave her to despair. But he had taken T.W.'s advice to heart and had come home to put his plan into action—one that would speak louder than words about how much he loved her. He wanted her to know she was more important than anyone or anything else in his life. He would give up everything and go to the ends of the earth, if necessary, to be with her.

"Maximillian." His father's greeting was accompanied by a smile that did not contain even a hint of displeasure. "You did not inform me that your wife would be joining us for our meeting."

"He didn't know," Emberly said easily, confidently, not appearing in the least intimidated by the king. "He came home to talk to you about our marriage, but I didn't want him to have to do it alone, so I had his assistant attempt to delay him as long as possible."

So that's why they'd detoured to the estate on the Bodensee, because Braun had been attempting to buy Emberly time to get to Karltenberg.

Max couldn't find his voice to enter into the conversation. It had gotten lost somewhere inside him, and all he could do was stare at Emberly as his love for her expanded within his chest, filled his heart, and thrummed through his blood.

Good heavens. This woman. How had he made it through the past two days without her? Now that she was here, standing so near, he felt life flowing into him again.

His father shifted to look at Emberly, the admiration for her beauty shining in his eyes. "I had the pleasure of sitting down with Emberly for the past hour and hearing all about her and how much she loves you."

Max nodded, which was about all he could manage. He had no doubt his father had investigated everything there was to know about the McQuaids the moment he'd heard the news about his marriage to Emberly, which had been splashed all over the internet and news not long after the press conference he'd had outside the ranch gates.

His dad had every right to investigate Emberly and the McQuaids the same way T.W. had investigated Max. Max hadn't heard anything negative from his dad yet, no texts asking what he'd done or demanding that he annul the marriage. Was it possible his dad had softened over the years and was more concerned about Max marrying someone he loved rather than someone with a title?

Or perhaps the few days Max had been stranded in the wilderness during the storm had put Max's situation into perspective for his father. Whatever the case, Max had felt a shift in attitude from his father since then. Perhaps almost losing a son made other issues appear more trivial in comparison.

Emberly was watching his face. "I think I've surprised my husband so much that I've made him speechless."

His father offered him another congenial smile. "That is truly a feat, for I rarely see Maximillian speechless."

"Then I guess I'll have to be the one to do all the speaking at our meeting."

"Perhaps so."

Emberly squeezed Father's arm, then released him and began to cross to Max. "I believe Max will make an excellent king. He's strong, decisive, and determined."

Something sharp in her eyes told him she knew about his plan to abdicate and that was why she had come—to stop him.

Max had instructed her family not to say anything to her about his intention until after the deed was done and he came back to tell her in person. Perhaps they had informed her regardless of his wishes. Or perhaps she had discovered his plans for herself.

Whatever the case, he could not let her interfere. "Father, what Emberly means to say is that I would have made an excellent king—"

"Will." Emberly spoke emphatically. "You *will* make an excellent king, and I'll be right there by your side helping you, encouraging you, and doing my part every step of the way."

What was she saying? Did she believe him that his motivation for marrying her was sincere? That he had not done so to gain the throne?

She nodded, as though sensing his question. "Not only are you strong, decisive, and determined, but you are also humble, sacrificial, and noble. Those qualities are important not only in a king but in a husband. And I know you will make an excellent husband too."

Before he could find his voice to respond, she reached him, stopped, and lifted onto her toes to press a kiss to his cheek. His senses were overwhelmed by her warmth, her softness, and her sunshine-citrus scent. He wanted to pull her into an embrace, lower his lips to hers, and taste her.

But she broke away and positioned herself at his side, as though that was where she intended to stay and she would not let anyone dissuade her. "Your Majesty," she said in a clear voice that rang with confidence. "I fell in love with Max deeply and passionately. Yes, my love may have happened fast and furious, but it is forever. I will never leave him, not now and not ever."

Max trembled inside. What was she saying? That she'd experienced the McQuaid legacy of love with him? She hadn't thought she'd inherited the legacy because she was a woman. But one way or another, she had taken ownership of it just as he had.

Father opened his mouth to speak but then closed it. Had Emberly rendered him speechless as well?

Emberly's smile widened as if she knew she had lassoed them both and was now in complete control of the situation. "I might not know much about royalty and being a queen, but I will make it my life's mission to know everything about Max and to love him to the best of my ability."

Father's eyes welled with emotion. He cleared his throat, then met Max's gaze. "I can do nothing less than wish you and your wife a lifetime of happiness."

No doubt his father had gotten reports from both Braun and Winzig, who had informed him of the joy Max had found with Emberly. Or perhaps Father was just relieved Max had gotten married and had decided not to be so particular. Regardless, Father had given his blessing, and Max could not ask for more.

Well, he could ask for one more small request. "Father, might I have a moment alone with my wife?"

"Of course." His father tried to remain somber, but his lips twitched with a grin. "I do think you will need more than a moment, however."

This time Max couldn't hold back a grin of his own. "You know me too well."

"That I do." His father's eyes remained warm. "I think you will need at least a month. Or perhaps two months for a honeymoon. Will that suffice?"

"I am not sure," Max teased.

Emberly released a soft laugh. "I won't complain."

"Good." His father laughed in return. "You both will spend the day here with us, meet with the queen and the other princes, then you will be off on your honeymoon wherever you wish."

Max gave his father a slight bow, hoping it conveyed his gratitude. As soon as his father left the room, Max turned to Emberly. He could not keep from gathering her in his arms at the same time that she launched herself against him.

Her lips found his eagerly and decisively, as if she were once again laying claim to him. He delved into the kiss with abandon, letting her wrap him up and tie him tight. Because the truth was, he had already been hers and would be forever.

25

Emberly's stomach pitched back and forth as if she were on a sailboat during a sea storm. As she lay in the enormous canopy bed, she tried to ignore the growing nausea, but it was getting harder with each passing moment.

Max had already left their bed some time ago. She couldn't really say when because she'd been so tired that she hadn't heard him leave. She had a vague recollection of his kissing her tenderly before going to his first day in training with his father to take over the duties of ruling the country so that his father could retire.

After two months of a blissful honeymoon, they had returned to the palace in Vollenstadt just yesterday in time for Max to begin his partial succession. His father would remain the king and head of state, but Max would become the prince regent and take over his father's responsibilities.

In anticipation of doing so, Max had taken time off from the bank and resigned as the CEO. He still wanted to be involved in the banking affairs to some degree, but he'd stated many times that his wife took priority and his country came next.

She leaned her head back on her pillow, hugged her arms around her chest, and released a happy sigh. Max made her feel like she was the most special person on earth. And in return, she'd tried to do the same with him.

The past weeks had been a delightful time of traveling around his country to his various estates, where they'd stayed a few days to a week before moving on to the next place. He had been the perfect tour guide, letting her experience everything his country had to offer. They had snowboarded, ice skated, sledded, taken moonlit gondola rides, danced all night at his favorite club, visited his family's museums, had bonfires on snowy nights, and so much more.

He'd taken her on his private jet to Paris to buy her wedding gifts. Another day, they flew to London so that he could take her to his favorite restaurant there as well as buy her more jewelry and clothes.

They'd mostly stayed out of the spotlight and avoided the paparazzi. But on the few occasions they'd encountered reporters, they'd managed to make that fun as well.

As much as she'd enjoyed all the activities and getting

to see his world and his country, her favorite days were when they stayed in bed all day, ate takeout, watched movies, and then kissed for hours.

Last night, when he'd held her tightly against him, he'd whispered in her ear how much he loved her. She'd whispered back that she wished they could stay like that in bed forever. He'd told her not to tempt him, and she'd told him she was mostly serious, and they'd laughed and kissed more.

Of course she missed her family and Colorado and the ranch. But a part of her knew she'd been destined for more than her life there, that she was a wild mustang that had needed to be set free to live her own life and roam wherever she pleased.

Thankfully, Karen had been willing to take over the event planner role part-time. And her best ambassador, Dwight, had been willing to fill in for the other half of the role until Tyler could hire someone else. She'd done her best to continue helping remotely, but the two hadn't needed her help much.

Tomorrow she would meet with the queen to begin going over the new duties, and she was looking forward to working again, especially now that Max would be busy.

She was still getting used to the lavish lifestyle, attention, privileges, and the servants waiting upon her every need. But Max had been protective and patient, teaching her what was expected of her at every occasion.

Now, as she turned over to Max's empty spot, she wished she could bring him back. Instead, her stomach roiled again. This time, the roiling didn't stop. She barely made it to the toilet before she threw up.

As she sat back on her feet and wiped her mouth with a tissue, she could only think of her dad when he'd first taken ill from his cancer and how he'd had trouble with throwing up. What if she had cancer too?

Tears sprang to her eyes—unexpected and totally unnecessary tears. But in the next instant, she found herself practically sobbing over an illness that she didn't have at the moment and probably would never have.

"Get a grip, Emberly," she whispered as she pushed herself up and wiped her cheeks dry. Her stomach gurgled angrily with a need for food.

Why was she so emotional? Why was she getting sick? And why was she so hungry?

As soon as the last question flew through her mind, she stared at herself in the wide vanity mirror.

No, she couldn't be.

Quickly, she calculated the passing of time and tried to remember the last time she'd had her period. She hadn't had one since before she was married.

She placed a hand on her abdomen. She was pregnant. There was absolutely no doubt in her mind. She didn't need a pregnancy test. Didn't need a doctor to tell her. She knew it deep in her bones.

A sweet, keen sense of joy overwhelmed her, and suddenly she was crying again, tears streaming down her cheeks, this time with happiness.

She needed to tell Max, but she didn't want to disturb him during his first day. Although she wanted to text him to come back to the bedroom right away, she somehow made it through the morning. She had her lady's maid discreetly bring her a pregnancy test and wasn't surprised when the double lines showed up, confirming that she was having a baby.

As the noon hour approached, she finally couldn't wait any longer to see Max and tell him the news. And of course kiss him again, because the few hours apart had been the longest she'd been away from him since arriving in Karltenberg.

She'd barely sent the text telling him she needed to see him when the door to their suites banged open and Max stepped in, clearly seeking her out without her beckoning. His eyes held a hunger that told her he'd missed her too. As he reached her, without a word, he picked her up, and she wrapped her legs around his torso and her arms around his neck.

Their mouths immediately fused in a heated, almost frantic need for each other. His kiss told her everything she needed to know—that he'd missed her that morning just as much as she'd missed him, that he didn't like being away from her, and that he loved her passionately.

He began to walk them backward toward the bed, kissing her with each step. When he bumped into the mattress, he turned and lowered her onto the bed while quickly covering her.

Before he could press fully against her, she broke the kiss, held up a hand, and stopped him. "Wait." Her voice was breathless but contained a note of anticipation.

He halted, his fingers spread possessively over her hips.

"I need to tell you something," she whispered.

He pushed back and studied her face. "What is wrong, darling?"

"Nothing's wrong."

He shifted to the bed beside her and propped up on one elbow so that he was looking down at her. "Yes, I can see it in your expression."

She smiled and caressed his cheek. He'd recently celebrated his thirty-fifth birthday, and when she'd asked him what he wanted most in the coming year, he'd said he wanted nothing more than a year filled with making memories with her.

Even if he hadn't said so, she knew he wanted a child—children—before he was too much older. Not just so that he could produce an heir but because he genuinely wanted to share the blessing of having a child together.

She slid his hand from her hips to her stomach. "I'd like to introduce you to someone."

Max's brow shot up, and confusion filled his eyes.

She settled his hand more securely on her belly. "Max, say hello to your baby."

He froze and held her gaze.

She nodded.

His eyes turned glassy. "Really?"

"Yes. Really."

He blinked hard, cleared his throat, then shifted so that his face was above her middle. A second later, he bent and kissed her stomach with so much reverence that tears stung her eyes too.

As he lifted his head, he finally smiled at her. "I love you, darling."

She plunged her fingers into his hair and began to drag him back up so that her lips could twine with his again and she could show him just how much she loved him in return.

Author's Note

Hi friends!

I always love a good prince story, don't you? I admit, the secret prince trope is one of my favorites! I do hope you enjoyed how Emberly and Max managed to find their fast, furious, and forever McQuaid legacy of love.

Of course, they did fall in love rather fast, and the wedding was also very hasty. I don't think it happens that way for most people, and I do think relationships can benefit from extended time getting to know one another.

But . . . I also agree with T.W. when he talked about the timing of relationships. Sometimes people date and are engaged a long time, but in the end their relationships fail. On the other hand, others have a very short "getting to know each other" phase, and they live happily ever after.

It's important to be wise in choosing that forever person. Once we do, then we commit to doing the hard work of making the relationship special, making it work, and making it last. Putting the effort into having a *quality* relationship matters more than the *quantity* of time together! And I do believe Max and Emberly are making their relationship one of *quality*.

So which McQuaid sibling's love story is up next?

As it turns out, Dustin was itching to have his story told. So those who are ready to read about Kade falling in love will have to wait just a little longer. Yes, Dustin, the silent and stoic one, is about to meet his match in the next installment, **Horseshoes and Honeymoons**. I hope you'll love his story as much as I loved writing it.

As always, I love hearing from YOU! If you haven't yet joined my Facebook Reader Room, what are you waiting for!? It's a great place to keep up to date on all my book releases and book news as well as a fun place to connect with other readers and me.

Until next time . . .

If you missed the other books in the Healing Springs Ranch series, then go read them today! What are you waiting for!?

Spurs and Sparks

Tyler McQuaid has been too busy managing his family's luxury ranch resort to think about love. But when his dad gets sick and may not have long to live, Tyler begins to question what is truly important. He's already failed once at love and marriage, but how can he say no to his dad's sickbed wish that he try again, especially with the feisty traveling nurse who causes sparks to fly?

Broncos and Ballads

After a bad breakup, country music star Brock McQuaid finds his ratings tanking as fans begin to question whether he's really experienced the love he sings about so passionately. To salvage his reputation, he agrees to pretend to fall in love with supermodel Venus Vargas, because she needs his help too. The power couple makes headlines, but how long can they keep up their charade? Or is it a charade?

Lassos and Lace

As the event manager for Healing Springs Ranch, Emberly McQuaid works hard to prove her worth to her family. When an international banking group arrives at the ranch and her best personal concierge falls ill, Emberly has no choice but to step in and assist their most illustrious guest, the young and handsome CEO, Max Berg.

Horseshoes and Honeymoons

Executive protection agent Dustin McQuaid is always in control of himself and is considered the best bodyguard in his agency. But he has one rule: Assignments to guard women are off-limits. When he's asked to protect the woman he once loved and hoped to marry, he refuses at first, but the large bonus might be just what he needs to launch the app he's been developing.

Find out where the McQuaid family began in the Colorado Cowboys series, a heart-warming, historical romance series. Join the McQuaid family as they seek new opportunities and find love in the wild and unsettled land of Colorado in the 1860s.

A Cowboy for Keeps

Wyatt McQuaid is struggling to get his new ranch up and running and is in town to purchase cattle when the mayor proposes the most unlikely of bargains. He'll invest in a herd of cattle for Wyatt's ranch if Wyatt agrees to help the town become more respectable by marrying and starting a family. And the mayor has just the candidate in mind for Wyatt to marry.

The Heart of a Cowboy

After watching his ma suffer and die in childbirth, Flynn McQuaid has sworn off women and marriage forever. Headed west to start a new life, he has his hands full not only taking care of his younger siblings but also delivering cattle to his older brother. He doesn't need more complications in falling for a woman he's determined not to love.

To Tame a Cowboy

Brody McQuaid is a broken man, and he knows it. While his body survived the war, his soul did not. Besides loving his little niece, his only sense of purpose comes from saving the wild horses that roam South Park. When the new veterinarian on the ranch turns her gentle healing touch on him, he's not sure that he's ready to tame his fears.

Falling for the Cowgirl

As the only girl in her family, and with four older brothers, Ivy McQuaid can rope and ride with the roughest of ranchers. She's ready to have what she's always longed for—a home of her own. She's set her heart on a parcel of land south of Fairplay and is saving for it with her winnings from the cowhand competitions she sneaks into. But her dream is put in jeopardy when the man she once loved reappears in her life.

Last Chance Cowboy

The repentant prodigal Dylan McQuaid is finally back in Fairplay. As sheriff, he's doing his best to prove to the town he's a changed man and worthy of their trust. When a woman shows up with an infant son he didn't know he had, Dylan is left with only complicated choices on what to do next.

Jody Hedlund is the bestselling author of more than seventy novels and is the winner of numerous awards. Jody lives in Michigan with her husband, busy family, and five spoiled cats. She writes sweet romances with plenty of sizzle.

A complete list of my novels can be found at jodyhedlund.com.

Would you like to know when my next book is available? You can sign up for my newsletter, become my friend on Goodreads, like me on Facebook, or follow me on Instagram.

Newsletter: jodyhedlund.com
Facebook: AuthorJodyHedlund
Instagram: @JodyHedlund

www.ingramcontent.com/pod-product-compliance
Lightning Source LLC
LaVergne TN
LVHW091715070526
838199LV00050B/2412